THE BIG RED HORSE

HarperTrophyCanada™
An imprint of HarperCollinsPublishersLtd

THE BIG RED HORSE

THE STORY OF SECRETARIAT AND THE LOYAL GROOM WHO LOVED HIM

LAWRENCE SCANLAN

WITH PHOTOS BY RAYMOND WOOLFE

The Big Red Horse
© 2007 by Lawrence Scanlan. All rights reserved.
Photos courtesy Raymond Woolfe.
Photos on pages 129 and 136 courtesy Lawrence Scanlan.

First edition

Published by HarperTrophyCanada™,
an imprint of HarperCollins Publishers Ltd.

HarperTrophyCanada™ is a trademark of HarperCollins Publishers.

HarperCollins books may be purchased for educational, business,
or sales promotional use through our Special Markets Department.

HarperCollins Publishers Ltd
2 Bloor Street East, 20th Floor
Toronto, Ontario, Canada
M4W 1A8

www.harpercollins.ca

Library and Archives Canada Cataloguing in Publication

Scanlan, Lawrence
The big red horse : the story of Secretariat
and the loyal groom who loved him / Lawrence Scanlan.

ISBN-13: 978-0-00-639352-8
ISBN-10: 0-00-639352-7

1. Secretariat (Race horse)—Juvenile literature.
2. Sweat, Eddie—Juvenile literature.
3. Race horses—United States— Biography—Juvenile literature.
4. Horse grooms—United States— Biography—Juvenile literature.
I. Title.

SF355.S42S325 2007   J798.40092'9   C2007-902237-5

HC 9 8 7 6 5 4 3 2

Printed and bound in the United States
Design by Sharon Kish

For all good grooms, everywhere

CHAPTER 1

HORSE OF THE CENTURY

▼▼▼

Every morning at dawn, at his "home" racetrack of Belmont in New York City, or at whatever track he happened to be, the Thoroughbred racehorse named Secretariat would stick his head out the stall door and wait for his pal. The stall had a strong door, of course, but the usual way of keeping horses in their stalls is to slide the door back into its slot and attach strong, foot-high rubber webbing into bolts on either side of the door set at the horse's chest height. This allows a curious horse to stick his head out, look down the hallways and watch everything. If a horse hears human footsteps or the clip-clop of another horse, he can check it out. Maybe say hello. Racehorses spend most of their time in stalls, and an open door helps relieve boredom. Early every morning, with sunrise still hours away, groom Edward "Shorty" Sweat would walk down that long hallway to begin his day's work, and every morning he saw the same thing. Secretariat with his head out, watching for, waiting for, his best friend.

Secretariat was a kind horse, and playful. Eddie would toss the horse's halter (a leather headpiece you can attach to a rope for leading a horse) into the corner of the stall. Secretariat would pick up the halter with his teeth and drop it at Eddie's feet; it was a game they played. Secretariat would try to steal the brush from Eddie's hand, and he would pull on Eddie's shirt like a pup playing tug-of-war.

Eddie was Secretariat's groom, the man who cleaned his stall, gave him his food and water, put on his bridle and saddle, picked the dirt and stones from his hooves, put on his blanket, loaded him in the van and drove him to the next track and the one after that. This was Eddie's job, and he did it better than anyone, according to many people long familiar with horses and grooms and racetracks. But looking after Secretariat was more than a job for Shorty Sweat. For him, that horse was like a son, brother and best friend all rolled into one.

Eddie knew, for example, that Big Red—as many now called him—hated to have his ears touched. He knew that the horse slept standing, facing a corner. At night, when the barn was quiet, the horse would lie down, but not on his side. He would fold his front legs beneath him and listen for strange sounds. When he heard one, he would quickly stand up. Ready to run if called upon.

When Eddie would arrive before dawn, Secretariat always stuck out his tongue. Eddie would grab it playfully and shake it as if he were shaking another man's hand. Ron Turcotte, the horse's jockey, or rider, started this by one day reaching into Secretariat's mouth and grabbing his tongue as a greeting. The horse must have thought this was another good game, because every morning after that, Big Red would stick out that big pink tongue of his, and Eddie would shake it.

"Hey, Eddie," Secretariat was saying.

"Hey, Red," his groom would reply.

This was their routine morning greeting through late 1972 and into 1973, when Secretariat was the reigning king of racehorses.

▼▼▼

How do you measure greatness in a racehorse? The most obvious measure is speed.

Think of land animals and speed, and you likely think of the cheetah, the lean spotted cat of the African plains. While chasing prey, the cheetah becomes a yellow-black blur streaking along at seventy miles an hour—the speed of one car passing another on a highway.

The quarter horse breed is also very, very fast. Some quarter horses have been clocked at fifty miles an hour. The mad-dash sprinter of the horse world, the quarter horse was originally bred to compete in the quarter-mile race, which is how it got its name. A quarter mile was the average length of a main street in the Old West, and nineteenth-century cowboys would race from one end of town to the other. Breeders were soon coming up with horses designed to win those wild cross-town sprints.

But neither the cheetah nor the quarter horse can make his speed last. Both are like kids in a candy store with their pockets full of change: they can't wait to spend it, and they do spend it—all at once.

We come now to the Thoroughbred racehorse. Thoroughbreds can fly along a racetrack at more than forty miles an hour, and keep up that speed for a mile or more.

Imagine the cheetah, the quarter horse and the Thoroughbred in a mile-and-a-half race. The cheetah would charge to a huge lead, then quickly fade before stopping altogether. The quarter horse would be right on the cheetah's tail, then pass him. But the Thoroughbred would soon pass them both and leave them eating his dust, with their tongues hanging out, their eyes rolling.

With his long neck and legs, his graceful sloping shoulders and powerful hindquarters, the Thoroughbred is the king of racing. And the king of kings was, and remains, Secretariat.

▼▼▼

Those who saw him run, whether in the flesh or on television, can never forget the sight. Just seeing him walk stunned some into silence. Those who knew horse conformation—how a horse's body matches the ideal of the perfect horse—could find no flaw in him. He was the most gorgeous horse and also the fastest. A few horses are stunningly handsome, and even fewer possess world-record speed. But until Secretariat, no horse could claim both qualities. There was also about him a princely air, of pride and grace and supreme intelligence, as if he were a creature gifted with speech but who, for reasons of his own, had chosen not to speak.

When Secretariat was feeling good, he would dance along in an easy trot, almost float—you would think he had coiled springs under each foot. When he was frightened, he would rear up on his hind legs and paw the air with his front hooves, and he would flare his nostrils and show the whites of his eyes. Eddie Sweat would let out the lead rope, beg him to come down from the sky and wait until the storm had passed. Then the horse would be calm again, his normal laid-back self, as if the whole thing had never happened.

Secretariat was a chestnut. Horses are often described by colour, and *chestnut* is the same red-brown as the nut that falls from the chestnut tree. Inside the prickly light-green casing is the nut itself, golfball size and so shiny and smooth you would think someone had spent time buffing it with a waxer.

But red-brown does not begin to describe the colour of Secretariat. If you were to take steel wool to a penny, and rub it long and hard, the penny would come up a brilliant colour, a rich, glossy blend of copper, gold and orange. That was his colour. Secretariat just shone in the sun, as if the light was not *on* him but somehow *in* him. Those who saw him up close often felt a powerful urge to touch him. Some did—before races, after races, one time *during* a race. A racing fan standing along the rail of the track that time did what one should never do—try to touch a horse as he gallops past. You could hurt your hand, or frighten the horse and cause harm to horse or rider. Maybe the fan obeyed some instinct that said, *He's a great horse. You'll never have this chance again. Go on, touch him.*

Horses are measured in hands, an old method of measuring based on the fact that the palm of an adult human hand is about four inches from top to bottom. Even without a measuring stick, you can get a rough idea of a horse's height by laying one hand above the other from the ground to the horse's withers—the high point of his back. Secretariat was sixteen hands, two inches (or about five foot six). He was, then, not especially tall, but he was two hundred pounds heavier and far more muscled than most Thoroughbreds.

The most respected racetrack writer in the time of Secretariat was an elderly gentleman named Charles Hatton, and he used to say that the horse "had muscles in his eyebrows." Some people believe that the Thoroughbred is the most gorgeous of horses, and that Secretariat was the most gorgeous of the Thoroughbred race. He had three white stockings (pure white hair above his hooves and partway up the leg) and distinctive narrow white markings on his head—a star and a stripe, as horse people say. In the world of showjumping, that white is called "chrome" (you'd think they were speaking of flashy cars). Secretariat had all kinds of chrome.

But more than anything, he had all kinds of speed. Charles Hatton once wrote that seeing Secretariat charge from behind during a race was like seeing "a hawk scattering a barnyard of chickens."

Imagine being at a racetrack and looking on as the great Secretariat charged out of the starting gate. Within six strides, a Thoroughbred racehorse is streaking along at forty miles an hour and taking in five gallons of air per second. Male or female, young or old, this breed of horse loves to run. Depending on the size of the horse's heart, the colt or filly may be pumping anywhere from twenty-two to forty-four gallons of blood per minute. (The human heart, by comparison, can pump almost six gallons of blood a minute if called upon.) The small rider sits on a tiny flat saddle and, because the horse is often very young and inexperienced (as young as two, and that's too young, say some), the risk of being thrown or trampled is there in every race. Thoroughbred racing is one of the most dangerous sports in the world, far more dangerous than hockey or football. Horses likewise risk injury and death. Yet the beauty of racing, and the excitement of racing, cannot be denied. You do not sit to watch a horse race. You stand, and you scream, and when Secretariat ran, everyone stood and everyone screamed.

This majestic horse raced what seems like a long time ago, in 1972 and 1973. There were no laptop computers then, no cell phones or iPods, and the breakup of the Beatles in 1970 had many young rock fans continuing to ask the same question: when would the Fab Four reunite? But more than three decades later, we still talk about Secretariat. And his owner and jockey get more fan mail now than they did when he raced.

This book tells his story. There is only one other horse mentioned in the same breath as Secretariat, and that's another chestnut horse called Man o'War who lived earlier in the twentieth century. We'll meet him.

We'll meet the fine and humble man named Edward "Shorty" Sweat, who served Secretariat as his loyal groom and who got closer to the horse than anyone else. The hero of *The Big Red Horse* is, of course, Secretariat. But Eddie Sweat dearly loved that horse and kept him healthy and happy. So Eddie, too, is a major character in this tale.

I spoke with many people connected with racing and Secretariat as I did my research, and all of them—certainly any who saw Eddie Sweat with Secretariat—would agree that the groom contributed mightily to that horse's success. Eddie was the one person he recognized and nickered to every morning. (A nicker is the sweet, low, repeated sound that a horse offers in greeting.)

A groom who worked next to Eddie for almost a year at Woodbine Racetrack in Toronto called him the best groom he had ever seen. Every night, this other groom told me, Eddie would cook up a hot bran mash for his horses. His horses' bandages were put on perfectly. And all his horses would stand quietly for Eddie while he hosed them down after a race or exercise. These horses, like Secretariat, loved him. He had a touch, a rare gift.

We'll meet this gifted horse's rider, Ron Turcotte (a French Canadian from a small town in New Brunswick), and Secretariat's trainer, Lucien Laurin (another French Canadian, born in a town north of Montreal). Both men formed a strong Canadian connection to this special horse.

By the end of the book, I hope you'll have a real sense of this champion horse and his world. The world of Thoroughbred horse racing has its own rich history, its own distinct language, its own rhythms.

For jockeys and grooms and trainers, life begins every day long before dawn, long before first light. Racing on Thoroughbreds is as close as humans can get to flying, and that makes horse racing both exciting and dangerous. The "sport of kings" is centuries old, and some horses' names are remembered in the way that certain old songs and hymns are remembered.

Secretariat is not just *on* that list of horses' names. He is first on the list. He was a horse who knew in his heart that he was the best.

CHAPTER 2

NEW FOAL AT MEADOW FARM

▼▼▼

12:10 a.m. March 30, 1970. When Secretariat came into the world, the world welcomed him with freezing cold, gusting winds and fog. He took his first breath in the little foaling shed, #17A, at the Meadow, a sprawling 2,600-acre farm on the banks of the North Anna River in West Virginia. Within twenty minutes, the leggy and wobbly foal was up on his feet. In forty-five minutes, he was sucking greedily on his mother's teats.

The Meadow was a classy horse farm. Its owner was a man named Christopher Chenery, and he had bought the land in 1936, though many in the horse business had advised him not to. Some said the pastures were too poor, the land was too wet, and it would never do for what he had in mind—a farm to raise the finest Thoroughbreds. Chenery was drawn to the land because his ancestors had owned it before the American Civil War, back in the 1860s. He must have felt a longing to get it back, to restore it to the family.

Christopher Chenery had money (for he was clever in business), he had a degree in engineering (which helped as he drew up complex plans to drain the farm's many swamps), and, most of all, he had a love of horses. He played polo and he rode every day. He loved the smell and look and grace of horses, especially Thoroughbred horses. The Meadow was his dream, and he lived it every day.

By the time Secretariat was born, Christopher Chenery was eighty-three years old and very frail. For years, the Meadow's horses had done well at the racetrack, but the luck had turned. A horseman *must* have luck. You can quickly lose your shirt by owning horses. There is even a phrase to describe it: *horse poor*. Veterinarian bills must be paid, and blacksmith bills. Medicines and grain and stall bedding must be bought. Fancy tractors are needed to groom the training track, big harvesters to gather the hay, and trucks to haul both horses and hay. Ropes and halters, saddles and bridles constantly wear out and need replacing. Such a huge farm required a staff of trainers and grooms, exercise riders and labourers. And though the sums of money from winnings at the track and the sale of horses seemed great, they could not keep up with the Meadow's ever-rising expenses.

Christopher Chenery's two daughters and son debated what to do. Should they sell the farm? Perhaps use the money from the sale to invest in the stock market? Finally, the youngest daughter, Penny, stepped forward and volunteered to try filling her father's shoes. She was a rider, she had studied business at school, and she had her degree. But would that be enough to pull the Meadow out of its tailspin? Her learning curve as the new farm manager would be steep.

"We'll need a miracle," one longtime worker at the farm said. On the night that Secretariat was born, that same worker called Penny Chenery on the telephone.

"Your miracle," he told her, "has arrived."

▼▼▼

Whenever the pairing of stallion and mare is thought to be a very good one, racetrack people call it "a nick." Hopes are high for the foal from such a pairing. And so they were for the new foal at the Meadow.

Secretariat's mother (or "dam," as she is called in the horse world) was a mare called Somethingroyal. A lovely name for a horse. As her name would suggest, her bloodlines were excellent. Somethingroyal's father (or "sire") was a fine runner called Princequillo. Some said his offspring "will run all day."

Secretariat's sire was a horse called Bold Ruler, and he was widely recognized as one of the finest breeding stallions of the time. He was a little accident-prone, and badly cut his tongue one time after a freak incident in his stall, and on another occasion he almost broke his leg at the watering trough in his paddock. Bold Ruler could also be *hot*—that is, wild and unmanageable. But the owner's wife, an elderly lady named Gladys Phipps, used to fuss over him and give him treats. After a race, she would lead Bold Ruler to the winner's circle, and he would walk peacefully alongside her, as one writer put it, "like an old cow."

Secretariat, then, had fabulous bloodlines. Bold Ruler colts and fillies were fast, but some people questioned whether they could maintain that speed. It was hoped that Somethingroyal, with her Princequillo blood, would pass on to the foal stamina for those longer races. Only time would tell whether the new foal was destined for greatness as a colt. But on one thing, everyone at the Meadow agreed. He was a truly handsome foal and he seemed to know he was a prince.

The farm manager who watched him being born kept a record of his first impression: "Big strong-made foal with plenty of bone."

Penny Chenery saw the new foal and wrote this in her diary: "Wow!"

Elizabeth Ham, Penny's secretary, commented on "his good straight hind leg, good shoulders, good quarters. You just have to like him." Secretariat's unusual name had come from Elizabeth, who knew quite a bit about horses.

In her younger days, she had worked as a secretary in Switzerland for an organization called the League of Nations

*Secretariat as a foal
and already muscled.*

(later, it became the United Nations), which in the beginning was called a "secretariat"—a word to describe people working for a common purpose. And Elizabeth Ham, the secretary, just liked the word. (Who can blame her?)

The name of every registered Thoroughbred horse has to be approved by the Jockey Club, which makes sure that no two horses share the same name. (Imagine the confusion if there were *two* Secretariats in the same race!) Elizabeth Ham submitted five other names—Secretariat was her last choice. But Scepter, Royal Line, Something Special, Games of Chance and Deo Volente (a Latin phrase meaning "God Willing") had already been used. No one, though, had ever named a registered Thoroughbred horse Secretariat, and no one ever will again.

▼▼▼

Time passed and the foal got bigger and stronger. Staff at the Meadow remarked on his personality. Out in the paddock, he was bigger than other foals his age and he used his size and strength to advantage. He already thought he was the boss, and he would play roughly with the other foals. His handlers had to be careful, for he was full of what we might today call "attitude."

One farm worker recalled that simply walking the young colt from the barn to the paddock required alertness, because Secretariat would make a dash for the grass the second his handler stopped paying attention. "We knew from the get-go," the worker said, "he was different."

Secretariat's dam, meanwhile, continued to baby him and attended to him for several days longer than normal. Maybe Somethingroyal was just that good a mother, or maybe she, too, realized he was a special horse destined for greatness. He was bright, he could be easygoing, but he had a temper, too. A complicated creature.

In October of that year, Meadow staff separated the foals from their mares. It was time for the foals to settle into a diet of hay and grain, time to end their reliance on their mothers' milk. This act marks the end of the bond between mare and foal, and there's nothing easy about it. It's a little like ripping off a bandage: you can go slowly, but that just prolongs the pain. The quick way is the best way, and grooms at the Meadow knew it. They took Somethingroyal and the other mares to a paddock about a mile down the road, so their foals could neither see them nor hear them. Back at the Meadow, Secretariat and the other foals were each put in a stall, a precaution in case they panicked. Some did, and tried climbing the walls. Some foals clued in, and accepted the loss of their dams.

But every foal called to his or her mare, hoping for a reply. And down the road, the mares did the same. And so it went all through that first night.

The young Secretariat pawed the ground in his stall and called out to Somethingroyal. No reply. You may wonder what he thought and felt about this sudden and awful turn of events. Can a foal who has lost his mother feel sorrow and sadness or fury? Does he keep the memory of her in his head, and, if so, for how long? Did Secretariat mourn the mysterious disappearance of Somethingroyal? Did Somethingroyal grieve her loss, and would she remember that spirited foal all her days? We know only that the bond between them was special.

In the morning, all the Meadow foals—for the first time in their lives—were turned out in a paddock without the security and comfort of their dams. The foals looked every-

where for their mothers, calling out and circling the paddock crazily. Still no reply. After several days and nights of
calling and searching, Secretariat and the other foals swal-
lowed the hard truth. They were on their own now.

▼▼▼

For the rest of that fall and into the following spring,
Secretariat did what young horses do. He played, he ran,
he ate. He loved all three activities.

Meadow staff were in the habit of putting the best young
horses in three particular stalls. The best prospect always
got stall number 11, and that's where they put the young
Secretariat. He had adjusted well to his new life without
Somethingroyal, and he grew attached to his groom, a
black man named Louis Tillman. In those days, and as
they had for centuries, horse farms and racetracks often
hired boys and men of colour. Louis was a foal groom, and
he cared for Secretariat and fussed over him like a grand-
mother would her first grandchild. Louis had looked after
countless foals, but he saw something in this young chestnut. Somethingroyal, he was convinced, had given them
something special.

In August of 1971, when Secretariat was coming on sev-
enteen months of age, the colt was slowly introduced to
the notion of riding. He had to learn about bits and bridles
and saddles, and about listening to a rider. A young horse
has to learn about the messages coming from a rider's

hands and legs and seat, and what all the messages mean. *Walk. Turn. Stop. Trot. Slow down. Gallop.* It's very much like learning a language, and if a young horse is asked to learn too much too quickly, he can get sour and lose confidence. Slow and easy wins the day, and that is especially true when the horse is smart and proud. A horse like Secretariat.

The bit and bridle came first. The feel of leather near the nose and ears and throat, the taste of metal in the mouth: these are new and strange, and some young horses object. But the Meadow staff were so skilled at this, and Secretariat so naturally calm and confident, that he accepted these new things and quickly figured out what was being asked of him. Then came the saddle. At first, his handlers would do nothing more than let young Secretariat experience the weight of a rider lying across his back, like a sack of potatoes. Then, in the stall, one rider would simply sit on his back. Again, the colt—who seemed wise beyond his years—reacted well.

Teaching all this to a young horse is still called "horse-breaking," and in the days of the Old West it was all done in a few hours or less. The idea was to break the horse's spirit, sometimes with spurs and ropes—whatever it took to teach a young horse that all his bucking and tossing would do him no good. He had to obey his rider, or else. A cowboy on a cattle drive might need to rotate four horses—a day horse, a night horse and two spares—and there was no time to school horses slowly.

Today, many smart trainers know that "horse gentling" is a far better way to go than horse-breaking. It takes much longer, but the horse gets to keep his spirit. He still has to obey his rider, but what the young horse should feel most powerfully during his education is trust, not fear. What Meadow staff wanted to avoid was a bad experience that a foal would never forget. They went slowly and carefully, and never put too much on Secretariat's plate on any one day.

Finally, late in January of 1972, the now muscled yearling left the Meadow. He boarded a horse van heading for Hialeah Racetrack in Florida. This was what the farm did every winter—drive the young horses south to continue their training under a warm sun and get them ready for their first races in July.

Secretariat knew a little about riding. Now it was time to learn about racing.

▼▼▼

A veteran trainer named Woody Stephens was on hand to watch the new horse being unloaded that day in Florida. The trainer had won the Kentucky Derby twice, and he had seen a lot of good horses in his time. "My God," Woody said, "that looks like a big old shiny red apple. He is absolutely gorgeous." He was, everyone agreed, pretty.

Pretty slow, more like it.

Secretariat loved his food, and he especially wolfed down his grain. He was getting chubby, and on the track he seemed

Secretariat loved his grain—every last bit of it.

like a teenager suffering through a growth spurt, bumping into doors and falling over his own feet. He had no interest in racing. Worse, he had a nasty habit of jerking to the left— hard and fast, suddenly and without warning—while being ridden in a walk to cool off after a workout. The result? The poor rider landed hard in the dust. Eventually, one exercise rider suggested a different bit, and that seemed to fix the problem.

Lucien Laurin, the Meadow's trainer, was not impressed. A short, white-haired man who had lived his whole life on and around horses, he had come out of retirement to work for Penny Chenery. Lucien must have thought that the Meadow looked to be headed for brighter days, with some promising colts and fillies. But the new chestnut with the fancy bloodlines seemed to be falling far short of expectations.

Lucien had an eye for a good horse. He was born near St. Paul, about eighteen miles north of Montreal. He rode horses on Quebec and Ontario tracks for as long as he could and then turned to training, where he showed an ability to work magic with even ordinary horses. Most people liked him. He was funny, and reporters always warmed to him. But those who worked for him got to see firsthand his temper. When he exploded, it was like a volcano erupting—with smoke rising, sparks flying, rocks coming down like rain. And then it would pass, as if the eruption had never happened. One time he fired an exercise rider and the next day acted as if it had all been a bad dream. The rider tiptoed back to work.

Lucien Laurin also managed a big Thoroughbred training farm near Holly Hill in South Carolina, and he had trained many horses in his life. He was one of the shorter folks on the Secretariat team. There are photographs that show Penny Chenery and Ted McClain (Lucien's barn foreman) next to Eddie Sweat, jockey Ron Turcotte and Lucien Laurin. Penny and Ted, especially Ted, tower over the other three.

Eddie was five feet four inches tall. Lucien was even shorter, and Ron Turcotte was the shortest of the bunch.

Penny Chenery was always grateful that Lucien Laurin had come along. He was, she said, the perfect trainer for a horse like Secretariat. "I never trained a horse in my life as hard as I trained Secretariat," Laurin once said. He said he had no choice. That horse ate, well, like a horse, and then some. Had Laurin not worked him so hard, the horse would almost surely have gotten fat. And had Lucien cut back on food, Secretariat would have been cranky and miserable. So he got to eat all he wanted, but he was also made to gallop farther, faster and longer than any horse old Lucien Laurin had ever trained.

I say *old*, and he *was* old. When Secretariat started to race, Lucien was sixty years of age. He had a full head of white hair and the wide, flat nose of a boxer.

Just before Secretariat came along, Lucien Laurin's son, Roger, was the trainer at the Meadow. When a better offer presented itself, Roger left. Before he did, he suggested to Penny Chenery that she hire his father, who had just retired. What a nice turn of luck that was for Lucien—to have, near the end of a long career, the greatest racehorse in history land in his lap.

▼▼▼

Early in the spring of 1972, though, the young horse was far from great. Lucien wasn't steaming mad about the colt's progress, but he expected more. Where was the speed this horse was supposed to have inherited? Wasn't he a special horse, the Meadow's "miracle" horse? Some barn staff started calling him Ol' Hopalong, and fears grew that he would prove to be a dud. He would not be the first great hope to disappoint at the racetrack, and he would not be the last.

Lucien's long red horse van took Secretariat from Florida to what would become his "home" track at Belmont Park in New York City. I say *home* because Belmont was Lucien's base of operations, from which his horses were trucked or flown to other tracks. Lucien continued to test the horse in morning workouts, and the horse went on failing to impress. But one morning in June, the trainer looked up from his stopwatch with a big smile on his face.

One way that trainers and jockeys measure a horse's speed is by asking the horse to go a certain number of furlongs (a furlong is an eighth of a mile) and seeing how long it takes the horse to run the distance. Red-and-white poles are set up alongside the track a furlong apart, so a trainer with a stopwatch can know precisely how fast a horse is going. Secretariat had gone five furlongs in just over fifty-seven seconds—and that's quick. Five furlongs in sixty seconds would be considered average speed, so this was a good fast workout. The change from sleepyhead to speedster was sudden. It was as if he had woken up one morning and said to himself, "Okay, no more goofing around. Let's see how fast I can go if I try."

Lucien rushed to call Penny Chenery on the phone. He said, "We have a racehorse on our hands."

CHAPTER 3

EDWARD "SHORTY" SWEAT

▼▼

The man driving Lucien Laurin's red horse van down the
highway was always the same man. It was an important job
loading and unloading those valuable horses, getting them
safely to their destinations, making sure they were comfortable on their journey and during their stay at racetracks
from New York to Kentucky. Lucien had lots of grooms to
choose from, but he always gave the keys to the big van to
one man—his best groom, his most trusted, and, by all
accounts, the best racetrack groom anywhere.

Edward "Shorty" Sweat.

They called him Shorty because he was, in fact, short.
But he was not, in any sense of the word, little. He had
powerfully built arms, especially his forearms, and he was
immensely strong. The amazing thing about Shorty Sweat is
that he never had to use his strength with his horses, and he

treated them as if they truly were "his" horses. He had what few people have: a natural gift around horses, a touch.

▼▼▼

Edward Sweat was born and raised near the small town of Holly Hill in South Carolina. The soil is sandy there, the land is flat, and people—African-American, most of them—try to make a living on their small farms. They grow potatoes and corn and cotton, peanuts and watermelon. When Eddie was a boy growing up in the 1940s, he would have seen on the backroads around Holly Hill what you still see today—tiny houses with tin roofs and rough wooden porches. The Sweats were poor, *dirt poor* as some called it.

Eddie was the sixth child of nine born to David and Mary Sweat. Eddie's father was of mixed blood. Like many people in this part of South Carolina, David Sweat's ancestors were slaves, but the blood of white pioneers and Cherokee Indians was also flowing in his veins. When Eddie was small, the family was too poor to afford a tractor, so a horse or a donkey would have helped with ploughing on the fifteen-acre farm. Eddie's father knew how to gather herbs in the woods to make potions for sick horses and how to make poultices (a kind of plaster to help heal horses' sore legs). Eddie would have learned much about horses and animals from his father.

Young Eddie would also have heard a language spoken by many of the black men and women in his community.

Eddie Sweat, Secretariat's groom, looking relaxed at the barn.

The language was called Gullah, and it got its start centuries ago on the many islands off the coasts of South Carolina and Georgia. This was the time of slavery, when millions of black people of all ages were cruelly taken from their homes in Africa, put in chains on sailing ships and forced to work on plantations an ocean away. On the islands off South Carolina and Georgia, slaves from the Caribbean and West Africa toiled in rice and cotton fields, but they had trouble understanding each other. So they created their own language—a blend of West African and English that continues to be spoken on those islands today. As slaves left the islands, they took the Gullah language with them, and it found its way inland, and eventually to Holly Hill.

As a boy, Eddie used to board a school bus that took him past Lucien Laurin's horse farm every day. He would have seen those lovely Thoroughbred horses grazing in their paddocks or sprinting around the track with exercise riders on their backs. That was what Eddie wanted: to become a rider.

Eddie got a little work at Lucien's horse farm, but his mother was not pleased—at all. She wanted him to stay in school. An education was the only possible way to escape the poor wages and hard life that black farmers faced in those days. When, as a boy, Eddie worked in the fields on weekends, his wage was twenty-five cents a day.

But the horses, not school, called to him. He got work on Laurin's farm after class and on weekends, and then he quit school altogether. Eddie's immense strength was put to good use on the farm: he dug post-holes; he walked horses to cool them down after hard exercise (they call it "hot-walking"); he worked for a time as an exercise rider. But riders should be light, and Eddie got too heavy and powerful. He started working with horses from the ground. With Lucien as his teacher, he took up grooming.

Grooms get little credit for what they do with horses. They are typically paid badly (though the pay is a far sight better than twenty-five cents a day, and young Eddie must have been thrilled with his wages). Eddie would have started work at Holly Hill Farm before dawn, and his job list would have been long.

- Clean the manure from the horse stalls and haul it away in a wheelbarrow.
- Replace the soiled straw in stalls with fresh stuff.
- Tack up horses (put on bridles and saddles), untack horses (take off bridles and saddles) and clean the equipment with saddle soap and beeswax.
- Put grain in the feed buckets, put water in the water buckets, put hay in the haynets. Scrub those buckets daily with soap and water.
- With brushes and cloths, rub the horses daily till their coats shone.
- Clean their feet with hoof picks before and after their exercise.
- Use a garden hose to cool them down after workouts.
- Blanket them when it's cold.
- Take their temperature if they seem sick.
- Clip their manes and tails.
- Tend to their wounds and sore legs.
- Talk to them, always. And love them, always.

Eddie loved every horse he ever groomed, even the ones who turned on him. Eddie had a simple philosophy when it came to horses. He believed that horses were intelligent and sensitive creatures and that whatever love you gave them was returned.

His way with horses came to him as easily as laughter did. He knew, without anyone ever telling him, how to calm a horse. He seemed to know what the horse wanted before the horse himself wanted it. He knew where each horse liked to be scratched. He knew what worried each one and how to make that horse breathe easier. He knew all this because he had taken the trouble to find out, by watching the horse very carefully and over a long time.

A horse will tell you what he likes and dislikes. If you scratch his ear and his eyes grow soft and he sticks out his jaw, he likes it a lot. If he stares at you and swishes his tail, he's saying *Don't touch my ears!* A horse, in his way, is always talking. His eyes, his ears, how he carries his head (high or low), his tail (stiff, relaxed, swishing back and forth): all are used to send out messages to other horses and humans alike. *I'm the boss,* the horse might say. *I'm worried. I'm sore. I'm sleepy. I'm sad. I'm happy as a clam. I'm cold. I want my stall. I'm feeling frisky. Play with me. My back is sore. I'm curious. Where are my pals? You wouldn't have a treat in your pocket, would you?*

Eddie would usually be responsible for four horses, and he had a little book in his head on every one—favourite things, favourite foods, the sounds that frightened the horse, the rituals the horse adored. Some horses, after a workout and after the bridle has been removed, like to scratch their faces on a stall door to deal with an itch. The horse likes the scratching, and the habit comforts him. Horses *love* routine, and a horse denied a good scratching when he has come to expect it will have cause to be cranky.

A cranky horse can be a handful, even dangerous. Some men and women who work on or around horses must wrestle with their own fear. Maybe a groom has been kicked and lost teeth, maybe a rider has been thrown and had his bones shattered. It happens almost daily at the racetrack. But Eddie had no fear. None. (He had had his fair share of bites and kicks early on, all right, but he had found a way to avoid them.) Eddie's fearlessness, too, was a blessing for the horses in his care. A horse can smell or sense fear in a human, and that fear can then make the horse fearful. The horse is thinking, *This human is worried about something. Maybe I should be too.* But a calm and confident horseman, as Eddie was, can make a horse also feel calm and confident.

Eddie Sweat brought to his work what he brought to life: a great and constant joy. Eddie was always smiling and laughing and telling jokes. On most days he wore old work clothes, but on race day, and especially for big races, out came the fancy clothes. Penny Chenery arched an eyebrow at them, for she thought them too flashy and not "professional." But Eddie loved his pants with the wild stripes and checks, his bright hats, his two-toned shoes—black at the front, white at the back. Eddie wore clothes the colour of candy, as if he were shouting out his happiness at being alive. People who worked with him, those who employed him, the trainers, jockeys and exercise riders in his circle, they all loved him. In the way that some flowers will turn to follow the sun as it moves across the sky from east to west, racetrackers who knew Eddie loved to be around him. Lucien Laurin's barn foreman said simply, "Eddie was a prince."

Before he had sons and daughters of his own, he was the favourite uncle to many nephews and nieces in South Carolina. The Sweat cousins scattered around Holly Hill loved to see him coming. He would tease those kids, and pretend to find coins behind their ears. He would distract a child, steal the food right off the child's plate and then turn away with an innocent look on his face. The kids would swarm him, leap on his back, wrestle with him. Some of the adults around Holly Hill called him Big Bubba ("bubba" is a word in the Gullah language that means brother), but the children found that a mouthful, so instead they called Eddie Uncle Big Bull. That was a good name for him. He was as strong as a bull but as soft as a cat.

Eddie knew that horses love to hear language, from idle chat to warm praise. A calm and reassuring voice comforts a horse, especially a concerned horse, in the same way that a hug offers warmth and comfort to a human. Working around any horse, Eddie always talked to that horse, sometimes in English, sometimes in Gullah. There's enough English left in Gullah that you might be able to understand some words, but the most striking thing about Gullah is its almost musical quality. The words seem to rise and fall, like notes in a song. Perhaps the strange language made

Eddie and Secretariat appear to be having a chat before a race.

the horses focus on Eddie all the more. Maybe the horse thought to himself, *I have no idea what this guy is talking about, but maybe if I listen hard, I'll start to understand. But until then, it sure sounds nice. . . .*

One of Eddie's first horses at Lucien Laurin's farm was a sour horse called Bold Marker. Few horses are bad-tempered, but some are: they have been mistreated or, on very rare occasions, they were born with a mean streak. Hard to say what lay behind Bold Marker's anger, but that horse tore Eddie's clothes with his teeth and bit him on the shoulder— so badly that he was scarred for life. But Eddie refused to lose his temper or retaliate. The horse served up nastiness and got kindness in return. Eddie healed Bold Marker's sore legs and got him back running on the racetrack.

Every horse looks for a worthy leader, someone the horse can trust and look up to. What horse, even Bold Marker, wouldn't have been impressed with a man like Eddie? Bite him and he seems not to feel the pain. Kick him and he just glares at you but does not strike back, and calmly goes on with his brushing and pleasant chatter. Many people at the racetrack watched Eddie work with horses and all marvelled at his way with horses and the magic in his touch. A new horse would start the day trying to bite Eddie's hand, and by the end of the day Eddie had that horse eating out of his hand.

When Secretariat came along in 1972, Eddie was thirty-three and a veteran groom. Eddie got to know each horse extremely well, and he could tell when they were off or ill or upset, whether they were tired or sore, playful or fearful. He noticed when horses ate less or more, whether they peed or pooped less or more. He noticed any changes in their sleeping habits, any stiffness in the walk, any departure from the normal. He noticed heat in the horses' legs and feet (which may be a sign of injury) or a change in the horses' body temperature (which may mean illness or fever). He could look one of his horses in the eye and know—as if the horse were speaking to him—that the horse was happy or hurt, anxious or calm, feeling good or weary. And Eddie would pass on all this information to Lucien, who would ease up on work or rest the horse if need be.

Failure to notice any small change in the horse's behaviour could have a terrible consequence, even end the horse's career. A wise trainer once put it well: "A good groom will make a horse; a bad groom will break him." No horse had a more watchful caretaker, a better lawyer or a better spokesperson than Edward "Shorty" Sweat.

▼▼▼

When the new crop of young horses was shipped to Hialeah Racetrack in Florida late in January of 1972, Eddie was there to welcome them. The new horse, the one called Secretariat, was assigned to Eddie. But the flashy chestnut colt didn't impress Eddie much when he first saw him. Eddie thought the horse was a clown, that he was clumsy and wild, and Eddie was happy at first to share the task of grooming him with another Meadow stablehand.

Eddie's main horse at the time was Riva Ridge, who was already a proven champion and destined to win the Kentucky Derby in May of that year. Eddie loved Riva and called him Peahead for his unusually small head. As for the new colt, Eddie had grave doubts he would amount to anything. But those doubts started to fade when the young horse took to the races and began to show his power, his heart, his desire. Eddie found himself connecting with that horse, and the better Secretariat proved himself to be, the deeper grew the connection.

There's a saying at the racetrack: "It's not what the people do to the horses. It's what the horses do to the people." That summer of '72, Eddie began to fall for that chestnut colt.

CHAPTER 4

SECRETARIAT'S WORLD

▼▼▼

Racetrack barns begin to stir at three or four in the morning, when most of the rest of the world is still fast asleep. The first grooms arrive, and you hear the sounds of horses whinnying for their breakfasts, water pails being filled, wheelbarrows stacked with hay rolling down the aisles. As 4 a.m. gives way to 5 a.m., the pace picks up a little. More and more grooms arrive with first light; the birds begin to sing as they feast on spilled grain; and then the exercise riders start drifting in at sunrise. Horses are tacked up and ridden in a walk to the track, more and more of them with every passing hour. You can hear the clip-clop clip-clop of hooves, the sweet sounds of horses whinnying and blowing and announcing their presence, of riders chit-chatting to each other as they go. On some racetracks at the height of the racing season, there can be hundreds of horses and riders out on the track. And just as there are traffic laws to help prevent collisions, there are laws for the racetrack, too. (You'll read about some of these later.)

This was the world that the young Secretariat entered when he began training for a career in racing late in January of 1972. It's a world that has barely changed since racing began in North America in the seventeenth century. Horses still gallop in the cool of the dawn—to avoid the worst heat of a summer day—as they have for centuries. Hot-walkers, grooms, exercise riders, jockeys, outriders, trainers and owners still do today what they did in Secretariat's time.

To understand Secretariat's world—the world of the racetrack—you should know a little about the track itself. A racetrack is shaped a little like a rectangle, but with all the corners rounded. Imagine a soft-boiled egg being pressed from above. From high in the grandstands (where you would sit if you were to watch a race), you can look down on the track and see each race's beginning, middle and end.

"They're off!" the track announcer will say, and the horses will charge out of the gate. Some people at the track bring binoculars, because the races often start at the far end of the oval. Races may start far from us in the grandstand, but they always end right in front of our eyes.

That first long straightaway is called "the backstretch." But the barns and stalls are located there as well. So "the backstretch" can mean two things: a section of the track that horses run on or home for the horses and some of those who look after them. "Shed row" is another name for the barns and stalls, so "the backstretch" and "shed row" can mean the same thing: home to the racehorses and all who call this area their place of work.

"The stretch," on the other hand, means the last part of the race—from the last turn to the finish line. "They're coming down the stretch," a track announcer will say, and we all stand and cheer on our favourite horses. Let's meet the men, women and creatures of the Thoroughbred racetrack.

THE HORSES: You may already know the various names for horses. A *foal* is a very young horse, either male or female. A *colt* is a young male; a *stallion* is a male horse of breeding age; a *gelding* is a "fixed" horse incapable of breeding. A *filly* is a young female; a *mare* is a female horse of breeding age. Whether the Thoroughbred is a colt or a stallion or a gelding, a filly or a mare, speed comes naturally to each one. These are horses born to run.

THE HOT-WALKER: In racetrack society, as in every society, there is a top and a bottom. At the top are the owners. They are always referred to as if they were royalty, and they are paid the highest respect. They sit in the best seats, wear the finest clothes and sunglasses, get interviewed on television. The more money they have, the more likely they are to be called "Mr." or "Ms." or "Mrs." Far from them, at the bottom of track society, is the lowly hot-walker.

After an afternoon race or a morning workout, someone had to walk Secretariat. He would have been hot and wet, and a sweaty horse must never be put back in his stall. He can "tie up" (get stiff and sore). Someone would have had to put a blanket over him and walk him for a half-hour or so until he was well and truly cooled off and dry.

It's boring work hot-walking a horse. Half a brain will do. The hot-walker might be an old man nearing the end of his days as a groom or exercise rider or jockey, and it's only a matter of time before age or illness will make even this work impossible. Maybe the hot-walker is a teenage girl or boy hoping to catch on as a groom or with dreams of becoming an exercise rider or jockey.

The hot-walker's wages are very low. He or she could make more money working as a clerk in a convenience store. "Home" at the track is a concrete box the size of a horse stall. Food is likely fast food bought at the burger joint near the track, or maybe something out of a can heated up on a hot plate.

On the other hand, the hot-walker is a member of race-track society. The hot-walker has the company of horses, steady work and a roof overhead. For those who ask little of life, it is enough.

THE GROOM: The groom is a step up from the hot-walker and is more readily seen as a member of the team, or "stable." All the horses belonging to a certain owner and all the

Two pals: Eddie and Secretariat.

people who work for that owner are said to be part of that owner's stable.

The owner—who may own just one horse or hundreds—pays the trainer to train those horses. The fee charged to the owner is so much a day, maybe $75 per horse, and out of that fee, the trainer must pay the barn foreman, the grooms and the hot-walkers. A groom may earn just a few hundred dollars a week, or twice that. There are cheap trainers, called "gyp" trainers, who pay as little as they can. And there are class trainers, who treat their staff and their horses with kindness and respect.

A groom, a good one anyway, gets close to the horse during the dawn-to-dusk days. Many grooms will actually talk as if *they* were in the race, not the horse. "I was up against Native Dancer," a groom might begin a story, when it was, of course, the groom's horse who was in the race. "I won yesterday," a groom may say, when, of course, it was the horse who won. With some good and dedicated grooms, the line between horse and human gets blurred.

Maybe you've seen pictures of those creatures the ancient Greeks imagined into existence. The centaur had the head, arms and chest of a man and the legs and body of a horse. Half-horse, half-human. Some grooms become so wrapped up in seeing life as their horses see it that they cross over to the other side.

When a horse wins, the groom shares in that victory in every way. The groom feels joy, gets a small share in the horse's winnings (usually 1 per cent of the "purse," or prize money) and can point with pride to his or her role in that horse's success. It may be a huge role.

Maybe the groom detected soreness and treated it before the horse got lame. Maybe he spoiled the horse a little, knowing that's what the horse needed. Maybe he taught the horse manners or to obey and trust humans. A good groom can work wonders with a horse from the ground, with the result that the horse tries harder at the finish line. A little more effort at the end of a race can be the difference between first and second place.

The good groom is invaluable.

THE EXERCISE RIDER: The exercise rider is one step higher up the ladder in racetrack society. The rider could be

*Exercise rider
Jimmy Gaffney
giving Secretariat
a workout.*

a former jockey too old for racing but still able to ride, or maybe someone who dreams of moving higher up the ladder and becoming a jockey. And while there are not many female jockeys, many women work as exercise riders.

Their job is to get the horse into shape by riding him in a walk and trot and gallop, to make him comfortable on the track and in races, to get him to listen to the rider and trust the rider. Exercise riders also report back to the trainer how the horse is feeling that day, whether he is energized or sluggish or distracted. If the horse is off, they might reduce his work the next day or rest him altogether. If a horse is feeling good ("feeling his oats," as old horse people would say), maybe they'd run him harder and longer the following day.

A horse cannot speak, but in many ways he never stops communicating. A swish of the tail, a little bob of the head, a shuffling of the feet as he's being tacked up: the horse is making a statement with all this body language. The exercise rider, along with the groom, must speak for the horse. But first they have to listen to the horse.

Exercise riders earn a decent wage, certainly a lot more than grooms and hot-walkers. And they face none of the pressures that jockeys face. No surprise, many of them really enjoy their work—despite the risks.

Every exercise rider has tales to tell of broken bones and awful spills ("wrecks," as they are called). A young horse who weighs almost ten times what a rider does can bruise and batter a small human without meaning to. A rider who falls from a fast-moving horse risks breaking bones, or being trampled by horses coming up from behind. The older these exercise riders get, the more they feel fear every time they ride.

Even so, exercise riding seems to put a smile on the human face. Now and again, a good or great horse comes along and an exercise rider can claim to have played a role in educating that horse. The rider won't get much credit, but when a young horse goes on to greatness, that rider feels a part of it. "I rode him, I shaped him," the rider can say with pride.

THE JOCKEY: It helps to be short when you're a jockey. Short may also mean light, and jockeys can't weigh much more than one hundred pounds. It's called "making weight" (staying at or under that weight), and jockeys struggle every day of their racing lives to make weight. They starve themselves, sweat in saunas and do everything they can to make sure they don't put on pounds, or even ounces. And though they may look little, they are among the toughest, strongest and bravest athletes in the world.

The job of the jockey, first and foremost, is to ride the horse in a race and, hopefully, to get to the finish line before anyone else. Jockeys can be old and young, male and female, English-speaking and Spanish-speaking, but their task is always the same: hear the trainer's instructions before the race, execute the plan as best they can, ride hard and fast, aim to be in the money. First, second or third.

Sometimes, before big races, the jockey will also exercise a particular horse in the mornings leading up to the race. The jockey can get a feel for that horse; the horse can get used to that rider. Horse racing is a partnership, and jockey and horse have to get along. And the good ones do.

When the jockey hits the big time, life is good. The money flows (the good jockeys naturally get the good horses and earn 10 per cent of the purses). Top jockeys have valets—personal servants to polish their boots, oil their tack and press their pants and "silks" (the jockey's shirt, whose colour and pattern the owner has chosen to represent that stable).

Sometimes there are parties after major victories. Stretch limousines may come around to the barn to pick up the jockey, the trainer and the owner. When champagne bottles are uncorked, the jockey is often toasted and hailed as a hero.

Jockeys just starting out have a different life. Young jockeys are allowed to carry less weight on a horse, so they have a little advantage against older, more experienced riders. On the racing program, a little asterisk goes beside the young rider's name—it's why apprentice riders are called "bug boys" (the term "bug girls" may be next, since there are now more female jockeys). Why *bug*? The asterisk (*) looks like a bug. Eventually, the rider wins enough races that the bug is taken away, but so is the weight advantage.

A lot of jockeys are looking for work. A lot of exercise riders want to become jockeys. So the jockey has to scramble, plead for mounts, charm the trainer, hope for luck. Many jockeys have agents to do the pleading for them, but then the agent takes 25 per cent of their earnings.

The jockey's work is exciting but even more risky than the exercise rider's. Exercise riders don't have to ride in tightly packed groups of a dozen or more horses, with horses sometimes bumping each other, every jockey wanting victory, every horse with his blood racing. Terrible things can happen when a jockey falls from a horse flying along at forty-five miles an hour, and every jockey knows what that feels like. The jockey doesn't dwell on what might happen. If he falls off, he hopes that the broken bones heal quickly, that when the cast comes off everything works the way it did before the fall. Then it's back in the saddle and into the starting gate, waiting for the bell to ring and the horse to charge out.

THE OUTRIDER: At big racetracks all over North America during peak racing season, dawn may see hundreds of riders exercising horses. Someone has to police them all to make sure they obey the little traffic laws that govern a track, and to rescue horse and rider when rescue is required. This is the job of the outrider.

The outrider lives a little like a firefighter. This looks like a sleepy job, and days can go by with nothing happening. But all that can change in a heartbeat. Any young horse who has tossed his rider feels overwhelming fear and panic. A powerful and deeply felt instinct to run takes over. In seconds, the horse can badly injure himself or another horse and rider. The outrider has to gallop hard towards that streaking horse, find the angle at which to cut him off, reach out, grab the reins and stop him. The job requires great skill, cool and calm from both the outrider and his specially trained horse, along with good judgment, balance in the saddle and a lot of guts.

At some tracks, a siren wails when a rider comes off a horse. Or, worse, when a rider is out of the saddle but with his or her foot caught in a stirrup while being dragged by the galloping horse. Most days, that siren wails at least once.

Accidents also happen during races, and again, outriders are always on the track—just in case. They are often former jockeys, and they have the respect of jockeys.

The major responsibility of an outrider is safety for all on the track. If an outrider spots an exercise rider who is clearly out of his league—perhaps because the rider lacks experience—then the outrider may order that rider off the track. Disobeying track traffic laws can also lead to a rider's being asked to leave.

There would be chaos on the streets if there weren't traffic lights and stop signs and drivers who obeyed them. The track, in the same way, has traffic laws of its own. A rider walking or trotting a horse must stick to the outer rail and move in a clockwise direction—the same direction as the hands of a clock moving forward. A rider in a hard gallop, on the other hand, must stick by the inner rail and race in a counterclockwise circle—imagine those hands of a clock moving backwards. A rider in a slower gallop must stay in the middle of the track but move in the same direction as a horse galloping on the inside rail. It's as if the track has been divided into colour-coded speed zones. The rider's

Left to right: A Meadow Farm employee, owner Penny Chenery, and trainer Lucien Laurin taking notes on the new crop of horses.

position—in the middle, on the outside, on the inside—always determines his and his horse's speed and direction.

The outriders are the cops who make sure that all riders follow these rules.

THE TRAINER: Decisions, decisions, decisions. The trainer makes hundreds of them every day. When will this young horse be ready to race, and where? Which race? Which track? How long should I rest him in the days after that first race? How hard should I exercise this young colt or that older filly? Which exercise rider is best suited to this horse? When will the filly be ready for her first big race—a "stakes race"—against tougher competition? What advice should I give the jockey about how to ride her? If the owner of the horse wants to run the horse in Chicago as a favour to a friend, do I agree? Or do I possibly risk my job by disagreeing? Do I stick with the jockey who rode her last time, or try another?

The trainer faces a lot of decisions, every day, for the many horses in his or her care. Make the wrong decision, and a trainer may ruin a horse or stall his progress. Start the horse racing too early or running against better or more experienced competition, and a trainer may damage a young horse's confidence. There's an old saying at the race-track: "Surround yourself with the best of company and your horses with the worst." It means that while humans at the track should seek the finest of friends, with horses it's the opposite: in every race entered, you want your horse to be the best of the bunch.

Good trainers come to understand both the mind and the body of each horse in the stable. Good trainers keep workouts fresh and interesting for the horse, and they surround themselves with good people: the best grooms, the best exercise riders, the best jockeys.

THE OWNER: When a horse wins a big race, everyone on the team shares in that victory. The jockey, who might be drenched in sweat or covered in mud, gets credit for guiding the horse home. The trainer wins praise for getting him in shape and for choosing the right race for that horse. The exercise rider can claim to have taught the horse manners and patience. Even the groom and hot-walker are supposed to get some bonus money, and they, too, can rightly claim that their work contributed something to that horse's success.

And while the owner gets to walk to the winner's circle, where he or she is photographed and sometimes interviewed on television, the owner can make only this claim: I bought the horse; I pay his bills.

And yet some owners *do* get close to their horses. Often an owner will go to one of the big horse sales in Kentucky and buy a yearling (an eighteen-month-old colt or filly). Some owners take a deep interest in their purchase. They research the young horse's bloodlines; they come around to the barn and feed their horse carrots. They watch him grow. They pin hopes on that horse, and some owners suffer when those hopes are dashed.

Some young horses get hurt, and the owner must wait while the horse heals. In the meantime, racing or no racing, prize money or no prize money, the owner has to pay the trainer. It's a rollercoaster ride, owning a Thoroughbred racehorse, and sometimes the horse an owner gets closest to is the one that offers the bumpiest ride. The owner cannot claim the same attachment to a horse that a groom can. The owner isn't there at dawn, wiping the horse's nose and the sleep from his eyes and feeding him his grain. The owner will never know the feeling of being on that horse's back in a flat-out gallop. The owner is seldom there for early morning workouts, as the trainer is, clocking times and watching the horse steadily improve, or not. The owner usually comes later, just before the mid-afternoon race.

You should have deep pockets—pockets full of money—to own even one Thoroughbred racehorse. Some owners have many horses and are sometimes resented for their wealth, just as hot-walkers are dismissed for their empty pockets. Welcome to racetrack society.

THE FANS: Most people who go to the track can't resist betting, even if it's just two dollars in the big race of the day. They try to pick the winner and make some money (though losing money is the far more usual outcome).

If you want to bet at a racetrack, you go to a clerk before the race, and you say which horse you like (his number, that is), which race (there are usually nine) and how much you're betting. The minimum bet is two dollars. Betting can get complicated, especially if you're betting on what order the horses will finish. Win, Place and Show, though, is all you really need to know.

A *show* bet is the safest of bets. You win some money if your chosen horse comes in first, second or third.

A *place* bet is a little riskier, but you win more money if your horse comes in either first or second, and you get two chances to win something.

The *win* bet pays most handsomely, but it's win or lose, all or nothing.

▼▼▼

The racetrack is like a patchwork quilt. Grandmothers used to make such quilts, using blocks of material from old dresses and pants, shirts and blouses. The colours and textures didn't always match, but all those colliding bits gave the quilt energy and every block of colour had a story to tell.

The racetrack, in the same way, gathers rich and poor, the schooled and the unschooled, and every culture and skin colour under the sun. What brings them together is the Thoroughbred racehorse, one of the most graceful animals on the planet.

Most of those horses will spend no time in the limelight. Most will lose far more often than they will win. Their lives may be cut short by injury or illness, and the humans who have power over them may be kind or not. In the book *Black Beauty*, a wise mare offers this advice to her foal: "I hope you will fall into good hands. But a horse never knows who may buy him, or who may drive him. It is all a chance . . ."

The track can be a hard place, where hopes and dreams are dashed—for owners, trainers, jockeys and grooms and all the others who make up track society. But now and again, a horse comes along and sheds glory in his wake. The one called Secretariat will never be forgotten.

Some racetrackers call what they do "the game." Those who play the game today all have the same wish—that one day another Secretariat will come along. They hope that they'll be there to see him run, to cheer him on, maybe to touch him. Only the dreamers dare hope they will ever own or ride or groom such a horse. It's been thirty-four years since Secretariat ran, and they're still waiting. They can only hope, and the track—for all its disappointments— is built on hope.

Maybe that hope has no basis. Maybe the Big Red Horse was IT. Maybe he was the best of a noble race of runners, one we must admire by looking back, for we may never see his like again.

CHAPTER 5

THE ROAD TO THE TRIPLE CROWN

▼▼▼

A young Thoroughbred horse—even though he has known human touch since being a foal—is afraid of all new things, and he may always be afraid of particular things that have frightened him in the past. Maybe a garbage bag blowing, twisting and circling in the wind that scared him half to death one time. Maybe a green garden hose, so like a snake and not to be trusted. Maybe a starting gate, with its harsh smell of metal, its cold touch, its loud bell.

In the spring of 1972, Secretariat was only a few months past two years old. In human terms, he was the equivalent of a young teenager—easily distracted, full of energy, a little undisciplined.

One day his exercise rider, a man named Jimmy Gaffney who had taken a real shine to Secretariat, was riding the colt in a walk after a workout at Saratoga in upper New

York state, one of the oldest and most treasured racetracks in America. It was early morning and there was a fine mist in the air. Up ahead Gaffney could see a man about to enter a truck, and he shouted at him, "Don't start the truck!" One sound the young horse feared, Jimmy knew from past experience, was that of an engine starting up.

But it was too late. The man was already inside and now he turned the key. The colt reacted. First he dashed sideways, and then he shot forward. All this in the blink of an eye. One of the astonishing things about young horses is the speed and thrust of their sideways motion, or "shy." Secretariat was so strong, so quick and so explosive that the force of his shy went far beyond the usual. Jimmy was an experienced rider who had been on tough young horses all his life, but not even he could ride out this storm. Jimmy found himself on the ground gripping the reins and being dragged, like a swimmer clutching a rope behind a speedboat.

Secretariat darted down the track, through "the gap" leading to the barns and onto some grass where, finally, Jimmy let go. One of the Saratoga grooms eventually got close enough to grab Secretariat's reins and stop him.

Everyone in the Meadow stable must have been terrified. What if Jimmy had been badly injured, or worse? What if the young horse had been hurt? What if he had run into another horse?

For all their power, young Thoroughbreds are actually fragile creatures. And their worst enemy is panic.

Secretariat at the age of two was already as big as a three-year-old.

▼▼▼

Secretariat's first race, on July 4, 1972, took place at
Aqueduct Racetrack in New York. The colt got bumped hard
by another young horse, one called Quebec. It was real contact, almost like a bodycheck in hockey. Only Secretariat's
great strength and balance saved him from hitting his nose
on the ground. What impressed a lot of people looking on
was not just the colt's remarkable recovery but how he did
not panic.

Although the bump slowed him down for a few seconds

and left him tenth of twelve horses, Secretariat went back to work and surged forward. The charge almost succeeded. He took second place and was only one and a half horse lengths behind the winner at the end. The race had been a short one; any longer and he would almost certainly have won.

The newspaper that reports on the world of North American Thoroughbred racing and race results is called the *Daily Racing Form,* and the *Form* later heaped praise on Secretariat. Its writer said he finished "full of run."

Less than two weeks later at the same track, Secretariat won. The *Form* had noted his bloodlines and his first showing and made him the favourite in this, his second race. He won this race by an impressive six lengths, and his jockey said the big colt "went past everybody else like they were walking."

On July 31, 1972, Secretariat raced for the third time— his first visit to Saratoga. By this time he had settled into a pattern. That bump in the first race had made him wary of horse traffic. A new jockey, Ron Turcotte, was now riding him, and Lucien Laurin's advice to the jockey was to let the young horse feel his way to the front. Laurin had been a jockey in his youth, and he had learned the hard way not to fight with horses. Some jockeys and trainers approach each race with a rigid game plan. Maybe the strategy is to save the horse's energy for a charge late in the race. Maybe the best tactic is to go to an early lead and hope to hang on at the end. Maybe there's only one horse the trainer is

Top: Secretariat (third on the rail) loses his first race after getting bumped early.
Bottom: It's a different story in his second race as Secretariat wins easily.

concerned about, and the way to win is to stick close to that other horse, wait for signs that he's tiring and then let the jockey decide the precise moment to accelerate. The horse, meanwhile, may have other ideas: maybe the horse prefers to charge to the lead and *hates* being restrained. Lucien Laurin liked to compromise, so that horse and jockey each had some say as the race ran its course.

Each race takes about two minutes, but jockeys must think it's the fastest two minutes on earth. "Use ton propre jugement," Laurin would say to Turcotte before a race (French was the first language of both men). *Use your own judgment,* the trainer was saying.

By this time, Ron Turcotte had ridden Secretariat enough in morning workouts to know how capable the horse was, how smart, how fast. Ron was inclined to let the horse decide, for the most part, the tactic in the race. Thoroughbreds, even as colts, race each other in their paddocks. The urge to compete is in their blood, and the jockey knew that Secretariat—more than any horse he had ever ridden—wanted to leave the other horses behind.

That day at Saratoga, Secretariat hung back. He liked to come from behind and charge from the outside. (Because a track is shaped like an oval, any horse sticking close to the *inside* rail of that oval covers the shortest distance. But many jockeys have the same idea—so the inside rail gathers the most traffic. By choosing to go wide to the *outside*, Secretariat had to go farther, but he had a clear path to the finish line.) At the same time, he had his ears tilted back—a sign that he was also paying attention to his rider. It seemed he was at least prepared to "discuss" with his rider another approach to running the race. But in this race, no discussion was required. The jockey allowed the young horse to decide strategy, and they won by a length and a half.

So far, no one could argue with Secretariat's tactics or his smooth running style. "He just floats," said Ron Turcotte after the race.

The jockey had grown up around horses and worked with them, even as a boy. His father cut trees for lumber in the forests of New Brunswick, using a horse called Bess. She was a mare, one of a distinguished breed of horse called the Canadian, whose history in French-speaking Canada dates back to the early seventeenth century. Young Ron loved that mare. "She was almost human," he once said. He would call to her and she would come, like a loyal dog. A typical Canadian horse, she was smaller than heavy draft horses, but she was immensely strong and could haul out of the woods up to 150 heavy logs a day.

There were eleven children in the Turcotte family, and jobs in 1960 were scarce. During a long period without work, Turcotte's desperate father sold Bess for $400—twice the going price for a working horse in those days. Ron was broken-hearted. He also saw no future in logging, and so, at only nineteen years of age, he went to Toronto hoping to land work as a roofer. A labour strike dashed that hope, and Ron got a job picking worms at golf courses during the night. Pickers crawled around on their hands and knees with a flashlight strapped to their foreheads and a tin can in one hand. It was back-breaking work, but it paid the rent.

One Saturday afternoon early in May that year, his landlord had the television on, and he invited Ron to sit down with him to watch the Kentucky Derby. A Canadian-bred Thoroughbred called Victoria Park was running in the race, so all across Canada many people were doing the same. (The horse came in third.) The landlord looked at Ron, who was the size of many jockeys, and suggested he try getting a job at the racetrack. Turcotte did just that. His way with horses helped as he went from hot-walker to groom, from exercise rider to jockey, but his ascent up the ladder was neither easy nor smooth.

Saddle sore is a term to describe the awful pain in your thighs and back from riding all day when you're not used to it. *Saddle sore* is like *sea sick*. The phrases sound mild, but what they describe is terrible to endure. Ron Turcotte was so sore after his first long day of riding that he couldn't climb the stairs to get to his room. But he hung in, his body adjusted and grew stronger, and every day he felt better than the one before.

Ron fussed over every detail of riding and racing. A jockey, for example, carries a crop (a leather stick used to tap or smack the horse to make him go faster). In a crowd of running horses, the jockey may quickly switch the crop from one hand to another. To feel comfortable using the crop in either hand, the right-handed Turcotte ate with his left hand for months.

One day he would ride the greatest racehorse of all time, and in many ways he was the right jockey for that horse. Ron Turcotte used the crop when he had to, but he rarely had to with Secretariat. He never fought with the horse, and often let the horse decide strategy—coming from behind, taking the early lead, or trying another tactic. There are many ways to win a race, and Secretariat would try them all.

▼▼▼

On August 16, 1972, there was another race at Saratoga, a stakes race—that is, an important race, one with a fat purse. The competition was stiffer and included a horse called Linda's Chief, who had won an impressive five races in a row. But Secretariat did the usual: he let the other horses fight for first while he cruised behind them, and then he stepped on the gas pedal as they all headed for home. This time he won by three lengths.

Ten days later, he did it again, again at Saratoga. Another stakes race, with a purse three times bigger than the last one. This time Secretariat waited until the halfway point in the race before he made his move. As he sped past the other horses, Secretariat went wide at the end. This outside route, remember, meant he had to cover more ground than the horse on the inside. Even so, he won by five lengths and set a track record for the distance.

All that fall, Secretariat kept on winning, and always in the same way: dramatic bursts of speed, often on the outside, and late in the race. He did lose one race, at Belmont, when track officials claimed that he had bumped another horse, one called Stop the Music, and this led to his disqualification. But it was a light bump (nothing like the one he had taken from Quebec in his first race), and many Secretariat watchers believed the ruling was unfair.

As the racing season ended that year and the red colt rode in Lucien Laurin's van to winter in Florida for a well-deserved rest, the *Daily Racing Form* had a welcome announcement for those close to Secretariat. Lucien Laurin was named Trainer of the Year. And his fine young chestnut horse was named Horse of the Year, an honour that no two-year-old Thoroughbred had ever won (older horses had always won it in the past). Somethingroyal's foal seemed well on his way to something grand.

▼▼▼

Late in November of 1972, Eddie drove Secretariat and other Meadow horses to Hialeah in Florida for a little rest before resuming training under a warm sun. The red horse got an even longer rest than normal because a minor injury was discovered on one of his front legs, possibly from contact with another horse. Secretariat was treated, and for the next two weeks he did nothing more strenuous than a walk. But by the end of that month, Lucien Laurin had him back to work, with a good mix, from day to day, of walks and trots and hard, fast gallops. By March 10, when Eddie took him back to Belmont—the track Secretariat would have seen as home—the horse was ready for the greatest test of all.

Every spring, the entire world of horse racing wonders who will win the three great races—"the Triple Crown" of racing. The famous races are held just weeks apart and only three-year-old horses may enter.

First is the Kentucky Derby, in early May, at that historic racetrack, Churchill Downs, in Louisville, Kentucky. Then it's on to the Preakness, at Pimlico Race Course in Baltimore, Maryland. And, finally, the Belmont, at Belmont Racetrack in New York City.

In the spring of 1973, Secretariat continued his winning ways, and the whispers began. Was this the horse who would win the Triple Crown, the crown that no horse had won for twenty-five years?

▼▼▼

Secretariat had come to enjoy racing, and he was finding new ways to win. He could still, with Ron Turcotte guiding him, come up behind a wall of horses and find a little opening. Some said he looked like a speedy ball carrier in football, slashing through openings. Other times he would charge to the lead and stay there.

After a race, he would often just keep on going. Most horses are out of breath at the end and are quite happy to gear down, from gallop to canter to trot to walk. Not Secretariat. He was like a runaway freight train, and it sometimes took two track ponies and an outrider alongside him to slow him down. (A track pony, ridden by an experienced rider, is paired up with each Thoroughbred horse before and after every race. These "ponies" are actually horses, and they are either laid-back by nature or older, and it's thought that their companionship serves to calm a worried or anxious racehorse.)

Back in his stall, Eddie Sweat would serve Secretariat a feast of grain and carrots and mash, and the horse would wolf it down. This, too, was unusual. Delicate Thoroughbreds often go off their feed after a race. No matter how hot it was or how hard he had worked, Big Red was always keen to know the contents of his feed pail. Every horse was Eddie's pal and got the royal treatment, but there was no horse like Secretariat. The friendship between Eddie and the big red horse operated at some other level.

"My baby" is what Eddie used to call Secretariat. He adored that horse, and that horse adored him.

Those who are wise about horses are convinced that some smart horses can understand what you're saying (some trick horses have been taught to understand two hundred words or more), and *all* horses understand tone. To a horse, a soft, reassuring voice must be soothing, like the sound of water gurgling in a brook. Some people think it doesn't matter what you say to a horse, it's *how* you say it. A constant babble from his handler—especially when the horse is worried or anxious—tells the horse that all is well with the world.

While babbling away, Eddie would brush Secretariat the same way every time. Start at the head, then down the left side, then down the other side, front to back. Brush in one hand, cloth in the other. Eddie would brush and rub, brush and rub, to the same steady beat. You would think he had a song in his head, and maybe he did. Chatting all the while to the horse, Eddie put up with Secretariat's antics. The horse would lift his head, drop his head, bite the brush, swing this way, kick that way, or lean into Eddie's body. The horse had so much energy, and he couldn't stop twitching and swaying. Maybe there was a song in his head too.

"C'mon, Red. C'mon, Red. I'm gonna brush you now," Eddie would plead.

Eddie was in his early thirties when he groomed Secretariat. But he had been working around horses most of his life and he could call on decades of experience. If you had asked Eddie what he did for a living, he would say he was a "swipe" who "rubbed" horses. He was, in other words, a racetrack groom—and in 1972 he rubbed Riva Ridge, winner of the Kentucky Derby. That win was like a stamp of quality on both the horse and his groom. A groom who could say he rubbed a Derby winner commanded respect and stood to earn top wages (though "top" for a groom is more like "bottom" for just about everybody else). Many trainers saw Eddie's genius with horses and tried to lure him away from Lucien Laurin. Eddie declined. Among his other qualities, Eddie was loyal to Lucien, who was almost like a father to him.

The track offers some men and women the company of gorgeous horses, and that alone may explain why many humans, once they get a taste of the track, find it hard to leave. They stick around despite some tough facts of life there. Owners fire trainers, trainers fire jockeys, exercise riders get dropped, grooms are often overworked and underpaid, and horses will suffer if the humans around them are hard-hearted. And while winning a race feels good, racetrackers soon learn that winning is rare. Losing is the name of the game most days, and a steady diet of losing can darken your spirits. But once in a blue moon, the track offers something so rare, so touching, you just want to smile or shout for joy or throw your hat in the air. That's what seeing Eddie with Secretariat did for those who follow racing.

Racetrack writers began to notice and talk about this horse and his groom. And that was unusual. The groom seldom got mentioned in racetrack stories, but Eddie did. Whatever divide separates human and horse, these two seemed to have crossed it, and you only had to see them together to appreciate it.

Although not educated, Eddie was an intelligent man who knew a smart horse when he saw one. The groom became convinced that Secretariat understood every word he said and that there was no horse in the world like him. Lucien Laurin's barn foreman once put it this way: "Eddie and Secretariat were like brothers. They were joined at the hip."

In 1973, Eddie Sweat thought he was the luckiest man in the world. He was groom to two fine horses, Riva Ridge and Secretariat. Given his humble beginnings, it didn't get much better than that.

▼▼▼

Two weeks before the Kentucky Derby, Secretariat was entered in a race called the Wood Memorial, at Aqueduct Racetrack in New York. For the horse and his jockey, this was supposed to be just a warm-up for the big race in May.

But in that race at Aqueduct, on April 21, 1973, Secretariat stumbled. He didn't actually stumble, but he did disappoint. He finished third, almost five lengths behind the winner. Some fans actually booed Secretariat as he left the track that day.

A good groom knows when a horse is off, and Eddie could read this horse better than he could read a book. He noticed that Big Red lacked his usual zip in the days leading up to the race, and exercise rider Jimmy Gaffney noticed the same sluggishness when he rode Secretariat.

Secretariat certainly voiced his own opinion. He was an extremely smart horse, and he told Eddie—as loud as he could and as best he could just before the race—that he wasn't feeling well. The young horse refused to accept the bit in his mouth, and struggled with Eddie for about five minutes. Putting a bridle on a horse usually took Eddie about thirty seconds. Secretariat simply wasn't up to racing that day. And Secretariat *loved* to race, so when he said no to racing there must have been something wrong.

And there was: a veterinarian had discovered an abscess, or infection, in the horse's mouth before the race. The cause was likely a burr in his hay. The infection would have made his mouth very sore and drained off some of his usual drive and energy. But neither the veterinarian nor the trainer considered the infection a serious matter, and both gave Secretariat the green light to race. It's possible they underestimated the impact of the sore.

Secretariat was a horse who liked his jockey to ride on what is called "a tight rein." He didn't want the metal bit loose in his mouth. During the race in New York, Secretariat was snapping his head back a lot. The bit was hurting his mouth, and he was objecting to his rider's usual hold on the reins. For days after the race, Eddie applied hot towels to the swollen inner lip. Secretariat didn't much like it, and his eyes grew wide every time Eddie doctored him. But, as always, Eddie talked to the horse to soothe and comfort him. Later, in Kentucky during the days before the Derby, the infection healed and Secretariat was his old self, bracing against the bit and running like the wind.

The loss at Aqueduct, though, created doubt in some people's minds that Secretariat had the right stuff. Not everyone knew about the abscess. So many times in the past, horses had come along looking like sure things for the Kentucky Derby, and they had lost. Or they had won the Derby and the Preakness and lost the Belmont. Maybe, some said, Secretariat was one of those horses. A flash in the pan, not a horse for the ages.

Only seven horses in history have won the Triple Crown. Each race gets progressively longer. The Derby is a mile and one-fourteenth. The Preakness is a mile and three-sixteenths.

Longest of all—at a mile and a half—is the Belmont. To win the Triple Crown, a horse must be a sprinter, capable of coming close to that quarter-horse speed described earlier in order to compete in the Derby. But the horse has to be a stayer, too—that is, gifted with enough strength and stamina for the Belmont, to maintain that speed over the first mile and then the half that follows.

Was Secretariat both a sprinter and a stayer? Did he possess both gifts?

▼▼▼

At this point, many racing experts saw Secretariat as a very good horse. Not a great one, yet, but already worth a lot of money. Even before entering her horse in the Triple Crown races, Penny Chenery had to decide his future. Continuing to race Secretariat was one possibility, but there were good reasons not to. What if he got hurt? Would the media circus continue if he went on winning? Finally—and this may have been the deciding factor— Penny Chenery was deeply in debt. Her father had died, and she had to pay a crippling tax bill of $14 million. No, retiring the horse and selling him as a breeding stallion seemed to her the best option. And the money to be made was far beyond anything Secretariat could ever have made at the racetrack. (His winnings over the years would come to $1.1 million.)

Early in 1973, then, while Secretariat was still in the

prime of his racing career, Penny Chenery formed a racing "syndicate"—a kind of Secretariat club. Once he quit racing (in the fall of that year) and became a breeding stallion, members of the club would all share in owning the horse. More importantly, they would own the foals that he would sire. To be a member of the club, you had to pay $190,000, and that gave you one share in the club and the right to bring your mares to Secretariat at Claiborne Farm in Kentucky for the rest of his days. You could breed more Secretariats. Or, at least, you could try. Chenery had no trouble at all finding people keen to buy shares, and when the dust had settled she had formed two syndicates. One, for Secretariat, brought her $6 million. The other, for Riva Ridge, took in $5.5 million.

These days the breeding rights to a champion racehorse sell for much, much more, but in 1973, that was the going price for a gifted horse and his fine stable mate. Members of the syndicate were buying Secretariat's future, and that future looked very bright indeed. Penny Chenery's money woes were a lot closer to being solved, for the moment, but the $6-million price tag only served to put more pressure on the Meadow team.

Each one had his own anxieties. Lucien Laurin, the trainer, worried about keeping the horse fit for every Triple Crown race. Working the horse too hard was as much a concern as working him too little. Ron Turcotte, the jockey, was also worried. If Secretariat lost, would the blame fall on him? And the groom, of course, worried more than anyone. For the next thirty-five days, as each event unfolded in the Triple Crown of racing, Eddie hardly left Secretariat's side. Sleep, when it came at all, came in fits and starts.

CHAPTER 6

THE KENTUCKY DERBY

▼▼

Even if everyone else was fretting about Secretariat before the Derby, the horse himself seemed very much at ease. Just before the race, on the afternoon of May 5, Eddie Sweat went to his stall to tack him up, but he had to wake him up first. Big Red was lying down in the straw and having a nice snooze. Race? What race?

Racehorses always know when it's race day because grooms cut back on grain the morning of the race and there's no early-morning exercise either. In the moments before a race, some horses are so edgy and nervous they break out in a white lather of sweat—something trainers never like to see. The horse is using up energy to produce that sweat, energy he should be saving for the race. Some horses refuse to enter the starting gate, especially before big races when crowds are huge and there's tension in the air. Secretariat, though, was always calm before a race, and the Kentucky Derby was no exception.

There was a great buzz that day. A record crowd of 134,476 people had come to watch the ninety-ninth running of the Kentucky Derby, the most famous race in the world, and to watch Secretariat, on his way to becoming the most famous horse in the world.

Home of the Derby is a racetrack in Louisville, Kentucky, called Churchill Downs, famous for its twin spires (like the steeples on a cathedral) overlooking the finish line. Kentucky has long been horse country and is known for its blue-green grass. Horses, of course, love it. Horse racing in Kentucky dates back to 1789, and Churchill Downs opened in 1875, when a chestnut colt called Aristides won the first Derby by two lengths.

In the early days of racing in the South, almost all the jockeys were black slaves. When Eddie led Secretariat towards the track that fifth day of May in 1973, he would have looked up and admired those twin spires as his ancestors had done before him.

Before the American Civil War (1861–1865), white landowners in the South bought slaves from Africa and used them to pick cotton in the fields, to do laundry, to cook and clean. And, of course, to groom their horses and to ride their horses in races. Sometimes black jockeys rode knowing that losing would cost them dearly: their white masters had warned them that a loss could see the jockey's wife and children sold, never to be seen again.

But this long, dark period in the lives of black men, women and children was not without its special rewards and satisfactions, for many learned the ways of horses.

In the first Kentucky Derby, almost every jockey was black. The grooms and stable workers would all have been black. The bond between black people and horses had started in the eighteenth century, and continued well into the twentieth century. Today, trainers still employ some African-American grooms, but they also employ men from Latin America and men and women from all over North America. But for a very long time, the vast majority of race-track grooms were black men from the American South. Eddie Sweat was walking a well-worn path.

The year before, Riva Ridge—Eddie's favourite, before Secretariat came along—had won the Kentucky Derby. Now Eddie was back at Churchill Downs, this time with Secretariat. Victory would put Eddie high up on a pedestal. He would become the first groom in history to "rub" two Derby winners in a row.

▼▼▼

Entered in the Derby was a horse called Gold Bag, who used to share a paddock at the Meadow with Secretariat when both were foals. In those days, Gold Bag left Ol' Hopalong eating his dust. Few expected that to happen in the Derby.

There was also a horse called Sham, a superb horse and the one expected to give Secretariat a run for his money.

Tension rose in the moments before the race when another horse, Twice a Prince, panicked in the starting gate while other horses were still entering. He reared up and fell backwards, and Secretariat and Ron Turcotte, yet to enter the gate, had to wait a full five minutes while Twice a Prince got sorted out.

Finally, the horses were all in the gate. Secretariat had to start from the tenth slot, more to the outside than Lucien Laurin would have liked. But that was the number they had drawn. Before the race, little numbered ivory balls were placed in a leather-bound bottle, and a track official shook them out one at a time. The first horse on the list of entrants got the first ball that came out of the bottle, and so on down the line. Luck of the draw decided starting positions.

The bell clanged for a few seconds and they were off. Secretariat charged out, then seemed to go on cruise control for a while. At the halfway point in the race, he was second. Ron Turcotte tapped him with the crop, not something he often did, but it seemed to wake him up. Your nap, the jockey was telling his horse, is over. Secretariat charged on the outside to the front and then drew mightily away from the others. One jockey, riding a horse called Shecky Greene, had a nice phrase to describe the experience of getting passed by the powerfully built colt.

"I glanced back," he said after the race, "and saw him coming and thought, 'If I get in his way I'll get killed.' He looked like the Red Ball Express!"

Sham, for his part, impressed by staying with Secretariat for most of the race, only fading down the stretch and grabbing second place. Gold Bag kept up with the leaders early on but then seemed to lose heart. He finished a miserable eleventh in the field of thirteen horses.

Secretariat's charge into the lead did not just look and feel fast. It *was* fast. The time of one minute, fifty-nine seconds and a fraction of another second (1:59 $2/5$, as racetrackers would write it) broke a record that had been set by a Canadian horse, Northern Dancer, in the Derby of 1964. Secretariat broke the record by three-fifths of a second. That may seem a slim margin, but when you're travelling at Secretariat speed, three-fifths of a second—less time than it takes to blink your eye—is equal to three horse lengths. That's twenty-four feet, or 7.3 metres.

The other remarkable aspect of Secretariat's victory in the Derby is that he did not lose speed as the race progressed. If you divide the mile-and-a-quarter race into five equal sections, you find that he actually got faster as he went. As the quarter miles flashed by, the track's precise timers recorded each one. The first quarter mile he did in 25 seconds and a fifth of a second. The next in 24 seconds flat. Then 23 seconds and four-fifths of a second. Then 23 seconds and two-fifths of a second. And the last one in 23 seconds flat.

Top: Secretariat is dead last early in the Kentucky Derby.
Bottom: Secretariat wins the Derby in record time.

Trainers just shake their heads when they see numbers like that. Most horses either hang back to conserve energy and then charge, or go out fast and try to hang on at the end. One strategy makes for a slow beginning and a quick end; the other calls for the opposite. Secretariat, though, was just smooth and steady. He was like a rocket lifting off into space, his acceleration increasing as the gravity of Earth was left behind.

The red rocket had only begun to soar.

CHAPTER 7

THE PREAKNESS

▼▼

The day after the Derby, a Sunday, Secretariat reminded everyone in his circle what a great store of energy he now possessed. He was a kind horse, there was no doubting that. He could demonstrate true affection, especially to Eddie, no denying that either. But he was also a performance horse, a stallion, and in peak condition, and now he couldn't resist revving up that immense motor of his.

He was so wired, so anxious to run, that Lucien Laurin gave exercise rider Charlie Davis instructions to tack him up and walk him so he would think he was going to the track. It was all Lucien could think of to settle him down.

Secretariat reared up on Eddie many times as he was being walked, and that must have been quite a sight—terrifying for some. But Eddie would just let out the lead rope, as if he were letting out the string on a kite, and then calmly talk the horse down from the clouds.

The next day, Eddie led Secretariat up an airport ramp and onto a plane before flying with him to Baltimore, Maryland. From there they took the red van to Pimlico Racetrack, just outside the city. The Preakness, the second jewel in the Triple Crown of racing, was just two weeks away.

The plane flying out of Kentucky was a special plane, a cargo plane equipped to carry precious cargo—like champion racehorses. Secretariat was placed inside a tall and strong wooden crate open at the top and almost as tall as he was, but not much wider. The idea was to protect the horse by confining him and leaving him no room to thrash about if the airplane's noise or rough ride were to frighten him. The inside panels of the crate were heavily padded, and Secretariat's legs were wrapped in thick and cushioned shipping bandages. He was like an infant all snug and secure in his blanket.

With him all the way was Eddie, as close to a security blanket as a horse could get. Whenever the horse flew, wherever he flew, Eddie went with him. Eddie would stand close by the crate, right by Secretariat's head. There was a haynet at the front of the crate, so His Highness could snack during his journey, and Eddie made sure it was always full, that the horse had water and, just as important as food and drink, the company of the man who loved him.

Once in Maryland, the Meadow team had to put victory in the Derby behind them and concentrate on the next race. For the Secretariat stable—owner Penny Chenery, trainer Lucien Laurin, jockey Ron Turcotte, exercise rider Charlie Davis and groom Eddie Sweat—the pressure was on. (Charlie, a childhood friend of Eddie's from South Carolina, replaced Jimmy Gaffney, who had had a major disagreement with Lucien. The trainer accused Gaffney of "showing off" on Secretariat.)

As before, a great many reporters crowded the track to get a glimpse of Secretariat. Racetrack media always followed every race in the Triple Crown, but now that more and more people had discovered the striking chestnut horse, there were more reporters than ever before. Many men, women and even children who had never watched racing were suddenly taking an interest. Secretariat now had a following, and they wanted to know more.

To satisfy that longing, a small army of writers and broadcasters from all over North America set out to see this wonder horse, record his movements and interview his owner, trainer and jockey. Even Charlie and Eddie, seldom mentioned in stories about Secretariat, were hounded in the way that rock stars and movie stars are chased and photographed. The pursuit would only get worse.

The horse was under a giant microscope. Some racetrack writers, for example, had grown curious about Secretariat's long and apparently effortless stride. Once he kicked into that high gear of his, he seemed to float past other horses, as if a strong wind were at his back, helping him and only him. It seemed like another wind was blowing hard against the other horses, especially at the end of races.

Let's measure that stride, someone suggested. So, at Pimlico in the days before the Preakness, they did. A New York track veterinarian, Dr. Manuel Gilman, got out his measuring tape after Secretariat had galloped over the freshly groomed track. At first, the result seemed less than expected. Native Dancer, a great horse from the 1950s, had a stride of twenty-nine feet, and many observers were convinced that Big Red was in that league. But no, his stride was just short of twenty-five feet.

Dr. Gilman had an explanation for his finding. Secretariat, he said, employed both a short stride and a long stride while racing, and they had measured the shorter one. He said he couldn't guess the long stride's length. Dr. Gilman called Secretariat "a most unusual horse. He's very heavily muscled and looks like a sprinter . . . but he also has the body length of the long striding horse. He's an all-purpose horse, a sprinter and stayer—and he uses the typical stride of each at different points in a race . . . The way he accelerates is fantastic."

Ron Turcotte agreed. He was astonished at how easily Secretariat changed gears. The long stride was for cruising. The short one was for short bursts of speed when he wanted acceleration. Then he might go back to the cruising gear, like the fifth gear of a car that saves on fuel. If Secretariat could ever be compared to a car, it wouldn't be a Toyota or a Chevrolet, but a Ferrari.

The jockey was astonished that so big a horse could be so agile. "Quick as a cat," he said.

▼▼▼

The day of the Preakness, Baltimore experienced the worst traffic jam in the city's history as racing fans flocked to Pimlico Racetrack. Almost 62,000 people filled every seat and packed the infield as well. A buzz ran through the crowd as each horse was introduced.

There was Sham, a good horse who had shown in the Derby that he could run with Secretariat—at least for a while.

There was Our Native, a solid third in the Derby.

There were Ecole Etage, Deadly Dream and Torsion. And the clear favourite: Secretariat.

The Kentucky Derby had drawn thirteen entrants; the Preakness drew just six. The Belmont, the next race in the Triple Crown, would have only five horses. Secretariat's next race in Chicago after that had only four. It seemed that every trainer had the same thought: Who wants to run against that big chestnut? Not me.

One trainer at least had a sense of humour about the impossibility of beating Secretariat. The trainer instructed his groom to take a photograph of the great chestnut horse.

"Just his head," the trainer said.

"Why just the head?" the groom asked.

"Because," the trainer replied, "all I've seen all summer—and all my horses have seen all summer—is his rear end."

Many of those watching at Pimlico that day were young "hippies" dressed according to the fashion of the day, the women in long flowing dresses and beads, the men with long hair, long beards and sideburns. They flashed peace signs and some held posters wishing Secretariat luck. He was not yet the king but everyone seemed keen to bestow a crown on him.

Secretariat looked eager for the race to begin. While Lucien Laurin was doing up the horse's girth (the thin leather piece under the belly that holds the saddle in place), Big Red kicked out with one foot and then the other. He was saying, *Hurry up! Let's go, I want to go!*

Strangely, the race started slowly. But within half a minute, Ron Turcotte decided to make a move on the outside. It was a spectacular charge to the front, and no horse could keep pace with him. The jockey just let Secretariat run.

And once again, another jockey was left trying to describe what it was like to get passed by that mighty colt in full flight, and once again the jockey likened it to being passed by a locomotive. George Cusimano, on Ecole Etage, said after the race that his horse was running along easily when they both saw a shadow coming. The jockey was sure it wasn't his horse's shadow, because this shadow kept

Secretariat leaves Sham behind coming down the stretch to the finish line in the Preakness.

on advancing. Cusimano said, "I got to hearing this noise beside me—them big nostrils goin'—and I knew what it was. When he came by, it felt like a freight train passing—blew the number right off my sleeve."

Secretariat won by two and a half lengths, and in record time. The *Daily Racing Form*'s clockers and several professional clockers on the scene all agreed on that fact, but the official timer didn't. Normally, times in races are automatically determined by cameras connected to clocks, but the massive crowd in the infield may have jostled the timers and caused them to malfunction. So Secretariat's time in the Preakness, though widely recognized and recorded by several independent and reliable clockers, would go into the record books as unofficial.

Still, Secretariat won, and won easily. There was no disputing that. One more race and he would have it. The Triple Crown.

CHAPTER 8

THE BELMONT

▼▼

Before the Kentucky Derby, Eddie Sweat had had a sweet dream. He told his nephew, also a racetrack groom, about it. "Looka here," he said. "I had a dream about the Triple Crown. We're going to win the Derby, we're going to win the Preakness, and we're gonna do something never seen in the Belmont. It will be totally unbelievable." (Notice the *we*, as if groom and horse had become one creature.)

On June 8, the night before the Belmont Stakes, Eddie had another dream. But this was no sweet dream; this was a nightmare. In his sleep, this is what Eddie imagined. Secretariat had a huge lead in the Belmont when he stumbled and hit the dirt, and all the other horses in the race went around and passed him. Somehow, Ron Turcotte stayed in the saddle, the horse got back on his feet, and they desperately pursued the others, but they never did catch them. Eddie woke up with his heart beating, his mouth dry. He did not sleep the rest of the night.

He wondered, Can dreams predict the future? And if they can, which dream could he trust? The joyful one, or that other one?

In the meantime, just performing routine tasks around Secretariat was becoming almost impossible. Uniformed guards were everywhere, all trying to keep crowds of fans, photographers and journalists out of the way. Tensions continued to rise at the Belmont barns that housed the horses entered in the race. Grooms and exercise riders and hot-walkers are used to working in the quiet dark of dawn. But there was no quiet. Secretariat seekers were all over the place, at all hours, and they were getting in the way. Fans came at dawn to watch the workouts, and many of them camped outside the racetrack the night before the Belmont to guarantee themselves entry in the morning.

Eddie just wanted the Belmont to be over. Maybe, he thought, victory will end the circus. The crush of adoring fans, the photographers' flashbulbs, all those TV cameras and their too-bright lights. Eddie always wanted, first and foremost, one thing: what was best for the horse. And though this particular horse liked attention and loved to be photographed (he would stop and pose, arch his neck, look proud and cock his ears forward whenever he saw a camera), there was a limit to his patience. Sometimes all he wanted was to be left alone.

Eddie was feeling the same way. In the days after the Preakness, Eddie had to treat Secretariat's right eye, which had become swollen when dirt got in there during the race. Normally, Eddie would dab on the ointment with no one about or just a few familiar faces. Now the gawkers were everywhere. It was like the horse and his handler were on a stage, and Eddie had had enough of it.

The time span from Preakness to Belmont was twenty-one days. Sometimes during those three weeks, Eddie would sit on an overturned bucket near Secretariat's stall and play with Scooter, the odd little twelve-toed kitten born in the Meadow barn on the day the horse had left for the Kentucky Derby. They had come to call him "the Derby cat," and he was seen as a good-luck charm. All his life, Eddie had dreamed of grooming a great horse, a wonder horse, and now that his wish had come true, he began to question whether he could stand the pressure. Some days, sixty journalists with notepads and microphones, lights and cameras would stand at the edge of the barn beyond the restraining ropes, waiting to pounce. There was no space, no privacy, no time for the comforting little routines that Eddie and the chestnut had developed in their time together.

On the morning of the Belmont, a hot and humid day, Eddie wore a red T-shirt as he led Secretariat from barn to tunnel to paddock. More than a hundred racing fans followed horse and man as they went about their preparations for the race. "Bravo," said some. "Bravo."

Some fans had found spots by the paddock rail that morning, and they stood there all day, ignoring the races taking place. Many races take place every year at Belmont Racetrack, but there is only one Belmont Stakes. All fans cared about that day was the eighth race, and the clear favourite. They wanted to be as close as possible while Eddie led him, and while Lucien continued the old tradition of the trainer tacking him up before the race. Finally, the call came.

"Riders up!" a track official shouted, and Lucien cupped his hands together, Ron Turcotte slipped in his left knee, and the trainer boosted the jockey up and into the saddle. Eddie's heart was beating hard, and he hoped his awful dream was just a silly thing that meant nothing, nothing at all.

▼▼▼

In the late afternoon of June 9, 1973, five horses came out onto Belmont Racetrack for the 105th running of the Belmont Stakes. The owner of the winning horse would earn a prize of $90,000. If Secretariat won, his owner could add that sum to the $130,000 already won in the Preakness and the $155,000 in the Derby—all this for running a grand total of six minutes and seventeen seconds. Secretariat's rate of pay would work out to almost $1,000 a second. But the money seemed to matter less to everyone than the trophy.

The sky was clear, track conditions were perfect, and the horses would be running against the wind down the backstretch. As soon as the crowd saw Secretariat, they began to cheer wildly. The noise was almost deafening, and some of the horses spooked sideways in fright.

Secretariat walked down the track in a pre-race tradition called the post parade. It's a chance to see all the horses and their jockeys as they walk one way past the grandstand and then the other, so everyone in the stands and watching at home on television can admire them. Secretariat was wearing, in a way, the colours of the American flag, red, white and blue. Red (copper-red) was the colour of his skin; blue and white (the colours of Meadow farm) were the colours of the blinkers at his head. The blue-and-white checkerboard pattern of Secretariat's blinkers was matched by the same pattern on his rider's silks. In a race, Secretariat always wore blinkers—a cloth that goes over the top part of the horse's head, with a hooded eyepiece so the horse can only see straight ahead and not sideways at other horses. Some horses worry about horses galloping beside them, and blinkers let them concentrate on just one thing: running.

By this point in his career, Secretariat didn't need blinkers. He certainly never wore them while training. But Lucien Laurin had noticed in the early days of the horse's preparation for racing that without blinkers, the young chestnut seemed distracted. With blinkers on, he seemed focused and more inclined to run. Lucien was a practical man and, like almost all racetrack people, superstitious. The rule was, *Stay with what works.* (Every time one of her horses raced, Penny Chenery would wear to the track a little pin—of a jockey riding a horse—that once belonged to her mother. The pin, she thought, brought her luck.)

Lucien didn't need to know why blinkers fired up the horse; he only knew that they did. Putting on the blinkers became part of the horse's pre-race routine: a little reminder that it was time for work. Time to race. The blue-and-white blinkers became the horse's trademark long after they served any practical purpose.

But even without the brightly coloured blinkers, many could have picked out Secretariat. For one thing, he didn't walk like other horses. He walked like he knew he was the best. He had bearing, and he walked like a king or queen strolling among common folk. Some of the other horses were acting up, bobbing their heads, fussing. They were being what horse people call "naughty" (they really mean "bad," but naughty is a nicer word). Secretariat, though, looked calm and confident.

Eddie once said of Secretariat, "The only thing he knows is eat, relax and run. He never acts up. He's always loose. Lots of times he'll look around at the crowd while we're going to the post, like he's saying, 'What's them people doing here?'"

Within minutes, the horses were in the starting gate. It was 5:38 p.m. when the doors all closed behind them. After a short pause, the bell rang, and the five horses charged out. At first, the race served up a head-to-head battle between Secretariat and Sham as the two of them sprinted side by side, the dark horse against the red, both running flat out. Half a mile into the race, they were still neck and neck, and many smart racetrackers were now thinking the pace was far too quick. Horses sprint, if they can, at *the end* of a long race, not at the beginning.

Penny Chenery turned to Lucien Laurin and said, "Aren't they going a little fast?"

"A *little* fast?" thought Lucien. Insanely fast, more like it.

By the one-mile point in the race, two-thirds of the way to the finish line, Sham was done. Imagine how physically spent he must have been, and how dispirited: Sham was a tremendous horse and, had Secretariat not come along, he would almost surely have won the Triple Crown. Sham had stayed with Secretariat in a flat-out sprint for a mile, given it all he had. But this other horse, incredibly, was pulling away, and Sham lost heart. He was behind Secretariat by seven lengths and fading fast.

The other horses—Twice a Prince, My Gallant and Pvt. Smiles—were nowhere to be seen. Secretariat was now racing by himself, and Ron Turcotte was just sitting on him, not using the crop, just guiding him. Whatever the backstretch wind that day, it was no match for this horse. With a quarter mile to go, he was twenty lengths ahead of the horse behind him.

Jockey Ron Turcotte looks at Secretariat's time near the end of the Belmont and he can hardly believe his eyes.

As they rounded the final turn for home, Ron Turcotte looked back to see where the other horses were. One newspaper ran a photograph taken at that very moment. The angle is perfect, for the photo shows Secretariat way out in front, his jockey turning back, and the other horses far behind. Below the photo are the words you can imagine Turcotte saying: "Hey, you guys comin' or not?"

By the finish line, Secretariat was an astonishing thirty-one lengths ahead of the horse behind. Twice a Prince, My Gallant and Pvt. Smiles finished, in that order, way back. Sham came in last, forty-five horse lengths behind Secretariat. He would never race again.

Secretariat and Ron Turcotte surounded after winning the Triple Crown.

Just before he crossed the finish line, Secretariat's jockey turned to face the racetrack timer, and a photographer took a closeup shot of the rider's face. His mouth is open and forming an *o*, that classic look of shock and awe. Ron Turcotte was an experienced jockey. He could sense precisely how fast a horse underneath him was going. Tell him to ride a horse a mile in two minutes and he would come in right on time, as if he had a clock ticking in his head.

But Secretariat was in that fifth gear, that cruising gear of his, and he had fooled his rider. Turcotte could not believe what he was seeing on that clock. Two minutes and twenty four seconds for a mile and a half, it said. A world record.

After the race, Lucien Laurin—the veteran trainer and former jockey—asked his rider the obvious question. Was there any gas left in Secretariat's tank?

Sure, came the jockey's reply. The horse was still fresh at the end of the longest race in the Triple Crown. "He could have gone faster," said the jockey.

Lucien Laurin just laughed. Secretariat had shattered a world record without giving his all.

CHAPTER 9

FROM HIGH FLYING TO HARD LANDING

▼▼

In the wake of the Belmont win, Secretariat's team basked in the glow of victory. They all felt a part of something grand. The owner, the trainer, the jockey, the exercise rider, the groom and the hot-walker: all now walked with a little spring in their step. For the owner and trainer, there were champagne dinners to attend and the pleasure of reading tributes in newspapers and magazines. By finishing first in the Derby, the Preakness and the Belmont, Secretariat had sent more than $374,000 to Penny Chenery, and, according to racetrack tradition, she passed on a 10 per cent share (or $37,400) to Lucien Laurin, and another 10 per cent share to Ron Turcotte, the jockey—who gave $1,000 each in cash to Eddie Sweat, the groom, and Charlie Davis, the exercise rider. "Merry Christmas," the jockey told them. Secretariat, without meaning to, had given them all something.

The plan after the Belmont win was to exercise Secretariat lightly, but he wanted no part of that. Eddie and Charlie would try leading him in a walk, but it was like a child taking a giant dog to the park. Eddie and Charlie would hold on for dear life as Secretariat led them this way and that way. He was saying, *I'm raring to run. Where's the race?* Most horses would have been happy to rest after three tough races in six weeks and all the travel, but Secretariat was not like other horses. He was tuned up and fired up.

Three weeks after the Belmont, he did race. In Chicago on June 30, he competed in the first running of the Arlington Invitational. Eddie, as always, went with him in the plane. The race was created just so the red horse would come, and while fans in Chicago were thrilled to see him (the mayor even proclaimed it "Secretariat Day"), trainers obviously weren't. Almost no one wanted to run his horse against him, and so Big Red and Ron Turcotte raced against just three other horses, winning easily by nine lengths.

He was well on his way to becoming the most famous horse in the world, for he was already seen as the fastest horse and, many agreed, the most beautiful. Eddie saw the horse from the ground, and he saw perfection in the horse's feet, which he proclaimed "one of the beautifullest set of feet of any horse I ever rubbed." With pride, Eddie observed that no chips or cracks marked Secretariat's hooves. "His are *smooth,* just smooth all over. But you know, *he's* perfection all over."

Eddie loved Secretariat's kindness, how he would use his teeth to pull on Eddie's shirt as a sign of affection, and how sensitive he was. Many Thoroughbred stallions are pushy and aggressive, and Secretariat could be that way, too, but Eddie could often make him mind just by raising his voice a little. If you spoke harshly to Secretariat, you risked hurting his feelings.

Now it was August 4. Secretariat was returning to Saratoga Springs in upper New York state to race on this track for the fourth time in his career. The chestnut speedhorse was still just three years old, what horse people call "a baby." Each time he had raced at Saratoga, he had won. And after winning the Triple Crown in such dramatic fashion, the whole world, not just the world of racing, was talking about him.

That August day at Saratoga was widely seen as a day to celebrate the risen star of racing. There were 30,000 people at the track. Even by Saratoga standards, it was an awesome turnout. They had all come to see Big Red, to cheer him on, to watch him win.

Hanging from lampposts all over town were pennants of blue and white, the colours of Meadow farm. The pennants were long, thin triangles, wide at the top, narrow at the bottom, and the white and blue were set out in a checkerboard pattern. The people of the town had put out flags of welcome.

To understand why a town would welcome a horse, you have to know that the early 1970s was a troubled time for the American people: the Vietnam War raged, and anti-war protests occurred everywhere. In one terrible incident in Ohio, four students—part of a huge gathering of what people of the day called "peaceniks"—were shot and killed by soldiers, and many more were wounded. The American president, Richard Nixon, was caught up in a scandal called Watergate, and though he denied being a crook and a liar, it seemed clearer with every passing day that he was. And as the investigation continued, more people around the president were also found to be guilty and unworthy of trust. The nation was desperately looking for a hero, someone to believe in, an honest face they could trust.

The rugged and handsome face of Secretariat that year landed on the covers of all the big American magazines— *Sports Illustrated, Time, Newsweek*—and all the major newspapers. At Saratoga Springs, someone with a shovel and a lot of nerve was selling what he claimed were Secretariat's droppings at $2 a bag. And the fellow had plenty of customers (until someone in authority decided that marketing horse poop was in poor taste). People in Saratoga wanted a souvenir of the great Secretariat—a hair or two from his mane or tail, a picture of him, a T-shirt, a pennant or poster with his name on it. The hero of the day was this racehorse.

Secretariat had what horse people call "the look of eagles." Some horses have an air about them. They don't look *at* you but *through* you. They hold their head high and look off into the distance, as if they can see things we cannot see or even imagine. Secretariat had that look. He was a noble horse who had crossed over from the almost private world of horse racing into the wider world. Just about everyone paused to take note of him.

And many of them were children. Maybe their parents had read them *The Black Stallion*; maybe they had ridden rocking horses at home or ponies at a stable close to home. Some parents wanted their children to see the horse so these young boys and girls could one day tell their grandchildren about him. At the time of the Triple Crown races, some restaurants in Kentucky would offer special menus with items (a hamburger, a breakfast dish) named after famous horses. In 1973, kids wanted whatever item bore the name of Secretariat.

Kids, teenagers, adults, they all wrote letters to Secretariat, and the farm in Kentucky where he lived after his racing career ended had to employ three secretaries to answer the close to two hundred letters that arrived at the farm *every day*. For most of his life, Secretariat was the star attraction: ten thousand visitors a year would come to the farm to see him, to photograph him, to draw him and, if they could, to touch him. Staff at Claiborne Farm must have grown weary, for every visitor had the same question: "Where's Secretariat?"

▼▼▼

Imagine being there, in the stands at Saratoga Springs on that early day in August of 1973, cheering wildly as the bell rings, the metal starting gates flip open and those five horses gallop out.

Thirty thousand people screaming can make a lot of noise. Everyone stood that day at Saratoga, and some of the younger fans had been hoisted onto the shoulders of adults so they could see over the crowd. Almost everyone there held in one fist what they were sure was the winning ticket.

In the rainy days leading up to the race, Secretariat looked to be full of fire: in morning workouts on a muddy track that should have slowed him down, he broke two Saratoga records. Longtime followers of racing, though, might have taken note of the fact that all the Thoroughbreds running against Secretariat on race day would be older horses. Onion, a fast horse with a solid racing record, was four years old, as was True Knight. West Coast Scout, another superb horse, was five, and Rule by Reason was six. Older horses can seem intimidating to a younger horse, but in the Whitney Stakes race at Saratoga that year, the youngest horse was Secretariat, and he was now widely seen as unbeatable.

That day, the Secretariat ticket bore the number 3—the number he wore in that race. Many people had no intention of cashing in the ticket. They wanted to keep it as a souvenir.

When the bell rang and the horses leapt from the starting gate, Secretariat immediately ran with the leaders, then dropped back to follow Onion and West Coast Scout. Everyone thought the same thing: Big Red is just cruising. Relax. At the final turn, Ron Turcotte had him up with Onion, head to head, and the jockey asked him to kick into that passing gear of his that had always served him well in the past. But to the amazement of everyone there, it was Onion who pulled away, not Secretariat. At the finish line, Onion arrived first—by a length.

It was Onion's moment in the sun. He had beaten the great Secretariat, but it would be his only claim to fame. Later, the two horses met in another race, and Onion finished well back. But on August 4, 1973, it was Onion first, Secretariat second.

All the cheering quickly faded. A summer snowfall would have been less of a surprise than Secretariat's coming in behind Onion. Why had he lost? What had happened?

▼▼▼

Secretariat was the favourite in almost every race he entered. Only in his first race, when he was a young, unproven colt, was he not favoured to win. After that, it was expected that Big Red would be victorious every time. In the Belmont, one of his Triple Crown races, someone bet $35,000 on Secretariat—to win. That's how confident the gambler was, that's how good Secretariat was. But favourites don't always win; sometimes the *longshot*—the horse least expected to win—comes through. Yet Secretariat was so far and away the best horse of his time, and maybe of all time, that the horse-racing world was shocked when he came in anywhere but first.

Ron Turcotte rode Secretariat in twenty races. Eddie Sweat was his one and only groom for most of the two years the horse raced. Many racing writers sang the horse's praises while he raced and long after. And all of them agreed that Secretariat should never have lost a single race in his entire career. Don't blame the horse. Blame the fever the horse was experiencing before the race in Saratoga Springs.

But why would a trainer ask a horse to run if the horse was feeling ill?

As another trainer later put it, "Sometimes a trainer thinks his horse is so good that even when the horse is not feeling his best, he's still better than the competition. So he puts the horse in the race, and the horse loses. That's human error, and should not be held against the horse."

Imagine all the pressure on the trainer—and on the owner. Five thousand people had gotten up at dawn just to watch Secretariat exercise in the mornings before the race. Another thirty thousand had come to the track on the afternoon of the race. Imagine their disappointment if Lucien Laurin were to say, "Sorry, Big Red has a cold. He can't run today. But you can always watch Onion."

Maybe you've heard the joke about the cocky boxer who told his opponent, "I can beat you with my hands tied behind my back." Lucien had so much faith in his horse—

"a super horse" many now called him—that he didn't worry about the opposition that day. Perhaps he should have.

The trainer likely regretted his decision. Some racetrack writers later wondered if the jockey should share some of the blame for the loss, but that seems unfair. And what about poor Eddie Sweat, who would have had to watch as the horse he loved went off to battle when he wasn't fit for battle? But maybe the greatest sympathy should have gone to Secretariat, who had to run when he wasn't his best and who had to put up with losing.

Horses know when they've won, and they know when they've lost. They know when the competition is better than they are, and they know when they're the best of the bunch. And Secretariat had no doubt that he was the best of *any* bunch. Sometimes he would graze at the track while other horses raced close by. Most horses—99.9 per cent of them—would at least look up as those horses passed. Many would spook, they would shy, run off to the side, maybe dance a little in a show of worry. Not Secretariat. He went on eating, for he was a brave and confident horse. A horse apart from the rest.

On the day of the Whitney Stakes, Secretariat did as he always did before a race: he stayed deep in the corner of his stall, as if gathering his focus in the dark for the work ahead.

As Eddie once said, "He's in the back of the stall. He knows and he don't want to bother. He's thinkin' about it."

After the race, Eddie led Secretariat back to his stall and the horse faced the corner. That's what the three-year-old horse did now when he lost a race, and he only lost a few. Penny Chenery wondered if he was pouting, when even Eddie couldn't cheer him up.

The jockey, though, had a different explanation. "After that race in Saratoga," said Ron Turcotte, "he was a very tired horse. He had a virus, and he was running a fever. He wasn't brooding over being beaten. He wanted to be left alone to rest and recover." The jockey was absolutely certain that Secretariat's few defeats were caused either by illness or lack of preparation beforehand. "That horse," he said, "must have been made of steel. The facts are there. He should never have lost."

CHAPTER 10

THE CANADIAN CONNECTION

▼▼▼

Less than three months after his loss to Onion, Secretariat ran his last race and retired from racing in November of 1973. Why, you may wonder, would anyone retire a young champion horse who has just *begun* to race and who looks unbeatable?

Imagine Wayne Gretzky winning the Stanley Cup and being declared the most valuable player in professional hockey in only his second year—and then hanging up his skates. We would never have seen the man we still call the Great One play all those years. It would have been a terrible loss. Some horses race a hundred or more times over five or six years. Secretariat entered only twenty-one races in the two years he ran, and he could have raced for many more years. He might have won several Triple Crowns and the biggest races in Europe. So why was he retired so early?

Because he was, quite simply, too valuable.

Secretariat could have won a lot of money in races. But he could make a fortune for his owner as a breeding stallion. And he did.

▼▼▼

After the Triple Crown victories, Secretariat raced just six more times. As word spread in the spring of 1973 about his retirement in the fall, more and more people went to the track to see him.

On June 30, he raced in Chicago, at Arlington Racetrack. Such a crowd (41,223 fans) had not been seen at that track in thirty years. He won, remember, by nine lengths.

On August 4, he raced at Saratoga, against Onion. We also know what happened in that race.

But Secretariat made a speedy recovery and won his next race, at Belmont, by three and a half lengths while setting a new record for the mile-and-a-quarter distance. Onion was in that race, and he was up there with the leaders for most of the race but faded at the end. It was Big Red's buddy from the Meadow barn, Riva Ridge, who put up the stiffest fight, but he proved no match for the sturdy chestnut. This race marked the one and only time that Secretariat ran against Riva Ridge. Eddie was still groom to them both, and it must have been thrilling for him to see his two favourite horses—both Kentucky Derby winners—running with each other for much of the race.

On September 29, 1973, Secretariat ran his first race on grass (he had always run on dirt) at the Belmont Racetrack. He wasn't actually supposed to run in this race. Blame the weather. Lucien Laurin planned to run Riva Ridge in the race, and Secretariat nine days later. But that plan was scrapped when the rains came. Riva Ridge always ran poorly in the wet, so Secretariat got the call. His first training run on grass had gone well, and that was cause for optimism. "He loved it!" Ron Turcotte said after taking him over the grass track. "I could ride this horse over broken bottles or a ploughed field if we had to. He adapts to anything."

But any horse needs time to adjust to a new surface, and Secretariat was not given enough time. In this long, mile-and-a-half race, he battled down the stretch, but he tired and ended up second by almost five lengths. Here was another loss that might have been avoided.

Sure enough, in the next race nine days later, again on grass at Belmont, Secretariat was ready. In the Man o'War Stakes, Secretariat showed what he was made of. Running against the wind down the backstretch, he cruised to victory in a time of 2:24 4/5. He matched the world record for that distance.

Eddie Sweat felt like he'd been on a rollercoaster. When Secretariat lost, the groom took it hard. When "his" horse won, he was the happiest man in the land. The bounce in Eddie's step was back now. Big Red was rolling again.

There was to be one final race. But where? Several racetrack managers pleaded with Penny Chenery to bring her world-famous horse to them (for he would fill the stands wherever he went), but in the end she decided that Secretariat's last race would be at Woodbine Racetrack in Toronto.

Why Toronto? Chenery explained to those who didn't already know that the horse's trainer and jockey were both Canadian. She also pointed out that a great Canadian horseman named E. P. Taylor—who owned a fine Thoroughbred farm near Toronto—had done a lot for North American racing. For all these reasons, Penny decided that Secretariat's final race would take place on Canadian soil. Or was it Canadian bacon that influenced her?

"Canadian bacon" is what Americans call a lean cut of bacon, which Canadians call "back bacon." And this bacon played a small role in the Meadow stable when tempers flared. During Secretariat's racing days, there were times when trainer, owner and jockey didn't see eye to eye. Penny Chenery and Lucien Laurin, especially, had some fierce battles, for both were strong-minded. But when the fighting stopped, as it always eventually did, they engaged in a ritual to seal the peace pact. Lucien had a little room on the grounds of the Meadow, and he would go to his kitchen and make up for Penny and himself a fine meal of fried eggs and thick Canadian bacon.

It now seemed that all that Canadian bacon had paid off. Secretariat's last race would take place on Lucien Laurin's and Ron Turcotte's home turf.

The homecoming did not unfold as planned. Just days before Secretariat's last race on October 28, 1973, Ron Turcotte was suspended by racetrack officials for something he had done during a race. Perhaps his horse bumped another horse and the jockey was blamed. He would be out for five days. Another jockey, Eddie Maple, was given the job of riding Secretariat, and Turcotte would have to watch from the sidelines.

The weather was what you might expect in southern Ontario in late fall: cold and wet. Still, 35,000 fans came out to watch the great horse race. Another 10,000 had come earlier in the week to watch his morning workouts.

Every morning that week, other grooms and trainers, exercise riders and jockeys would all line the fences by the track at Woodbine just to catch a glimpse of him. They all knew they were getting a rare chance to watch the greatest racehorse who ever lived. Every morning, as Eddie led Secretariat to and from the track, they would pass this honour guard. The men and women of Woodbine racetrack were showing respect for the horse, of course, but for his groom as well. These were the last days of that magnificent pairing, and what everyone felt was a powerful blend of sadness and awe.

On the day of the race, fans cheered the moment they saw Secretariat, and they went on cheering long after he dashed across the finish line almost six lengths ahead of

Secretariat wearing the maple leaf after winning his last race—in Toronto.

the horse behind him. A Canadian-bred Thoroughbred called Kennedy Road bumped Secretariat twice early in the race, and Eddie Maple said after the race that his horse didn't much like it. Acting on his own and without any urging by his jockey, Secretariat just took off, as if angered by this insult.

A fan later went out onto the track and scooped up as a souvenir some dirt at the spot that he reckoned was the magnificent horse's last step in the race. Secretariat's racing days were over. The record would show sixteen wins, three second-place finishes (including a disqualification), one third-place finish and one fourth. But he should never

Top: *Young fans bid fond farewell on Secretariat Day in New York on November 6, 1973.*

Bottom: *The team—Lucien Laurin, Penny Chenery, Eddie Sweat, Ron Turcotte, and Secretariat—pose one final time.*

have lost a race. Take away human error or bad judgment plus that bump in his first race, and his record would be as perfect as he was.

▼▼▼

The day after the race at Woodbine, Secretariat was shipped back to Belmont. He got light exercise every day through those last days of October and into November. The hard morning gallops were all but over, and maybe he sensed what all those around him knew. For Eddie Sweat, especially, the dream was about to end.

Secretariat appeared one more time on a racetrack. This was at Aqueduct in New York on November 6, 1973, and it offered 33,000 racing fans a chance to say goodbye to a much-loved horse. A black-and-white photograph taken that day—"Farewell to Secretariat" Day—captures the mood of farewell. Two young girls, maybe ten years old, stand at a chainlink fence. Both girls are clutching a sign half as big as they are, with the blue-and-white Meadow check in all four corners and, in the centre, these words: "Goodbye Secretariat. We Love You." The horse they called "the people's horse" would race no more.

The thought seemed not to please him. Ron Turcotte trotted him out onto the track and into the winner's circle, but Secretariat appeared angry that there would be no racing. He tried to eat the bouquet of roses that Penny Chenery held in her hands.

Another photograph shows Secretariat being led away by Eddie Sweat. Eddie's best friend, the exercise rider Charlie Davis, is up on his horse Billy Silver (the gelding adored Secretariat as much as Eddie did), and they are walking alongside. They are all heading west towards the setting sun, and Eddie has his hands up on the red horse's back. He's patting him, and Secretariat has his head turned towards Eddie, as if he were listening, and understanding every word.

CHAPTER 11

FOND FAREWELL

▼▼▼

For two years, Eddie Sweat had been Secretariat's closest friend. Eddie had cut the horse's hair; he had bathed
him (even his private parts, an act that required both
care and courage); he had nursed him when he was sick,
hand-grazed him, driven him up and down the East Coast.
Before big races, Eddie had slept outside, and even inside,
Secretariat's stall to make sure he was safe. Eddie loved his
horse, loved him like a son.

And this made Sunday, November 11, 1973, one of the
hardest days of Eddie's life. On that day he had to hand the
horse over to new caretakers at Claiborne Farm near Paris,
Kentucky.

Everyone in Secretariat's circle was in tears. Charlie Davis,
his exercise rider, just went to his little bunk at Belmont

Racetrack and sat silently on the bed. Charlie later stood up and peeked through the curtains just in time to see Ron Turcotte kiss Secretariat on the nose before the horse entered the van. Lucien Laurin was crying. Penny Chenery was choked up with emotion. The great run was over. But no one took the loss of Secretariat harder than Eddie Sweat. Secretariat really was *his* horse, and no one else could make that claim.

Eddie had a bad cold and a fever that day, and he felt awful anyway for having to part with his "baby." But Penny asked him if he would accompany Secretariat on the plane, and of course he said yes. Eddie loaded the horse onto the red van, and they drove out to the New York airport before boarding a plane bound for Kentucky.

Photographer Ray Woolfe was on the plane, and he took a remarkable shot. The photograph tells you all you need to know about the bond between that horse and that man. They are face to face. Eddie is leaning into the horse, and you can see by the look in Secretariat's eye that he's worried about something. Maybe it's the roar of the plane's engines or maybe air pockets outside are causing the plane to dip and shudder. The horse is using his teeth to grip Eddie's jacket, like a baby clutching his blanket. Eddie has his eyes closed, and he looks to be breathing in the horse. Maybe he wants the moment to last forever.

Eddie later told a friend, "This is a hurting thing to me. I'm so sad I didn't want to bring him over here. It's been

*Top: Eddie keeps a close
eye on Secretariat on
the flight to Kentucky.*

*Bottom: Worried as
the plane takes off,
Secretariat grips Eddie's
jacket for comfort.*

a wonderful two years. Now it seems like my whole career has ended." He was only thirty-four years old.

After the plane landed in Lexington, Eddie led Secretariat down the ramp. Penny Chenery and Lucien Laurin had tried to keep secret the date and time of his arrival, but word leaked out anyway. A crowd of several hundred fans and photographers had come out to welcome the horse to the state of Kentucky on this bright and cool fall day. A horse van took Secretariat to Claiborne Farm, some eighteen miles northwest of Lexington.

A new handler, a tall white man named Lawrence Robinson, led the horse to his new stall. But as he was being led, Secretariat looked over at Eddie. The new handler was a fine and experienced horseman, for this was a classy farm, and he would be Secretariat's groom for many years to come. Not long before he died, Lawrence Robinson would say that of all the horses he cared for in a life spent among them, he loved only one, and that horse was Secretariat. And he would say how sure he was that the horse loved him back, that he could see the love in the horse's eyes. But on that day, Secretariat did not want a new handler. He wanted his Eddie.

The muscled copper horse swung around and caught Lawrence Robinson with a kick in the bum—as if to say, *Eddie, who is this new guy? Why aren't you leading me?*

Eddie stayed on at Claiborne for another week to help Secretariat adjust to his new home and new handlers.

When the mighty chestnut was just a foal, he was weaned off Somethingroyal. Now he was being weaned off Edward "Shorty" Sweat. With each passing day, Eddie did a little less for Secretariat, and Lawrence a little more.

Eddie educated the new handler on what his horse liked and didn't like. Eddie informed Robinson, for example, that Secretariat didn't just like to be fed first before any other horse in the barn—he *insisted* on it.

Horses tend to be fed their grain at the same time, morning and evening, and they seem to have a clock in their heads that lets them know when it's one minute past the appointed time. A polite or shy horse may whinny to *ask* for his grain. An impatient horse may paw the floor to *tell* you it's time. And a proud horse who thinks he's king of the barn may loudly hammer the wall of his stall with one of his hooves (imagine the sound of a gun going off) and *demand* his grain.

Secretariat, Eddie told Lawrence, believed he was king of his barn, and of every barn that ever was or ever would be. He was not a humble horse. When he thought it was time to go for a run on the racetrack or for his morning grain or mid-day carrots or evening hot bran mash, he would let Eddie and everyone else in the barn know. The walls would tremble.

Eddie talked at length about the big red horse, and Lawrence listened. Like a worried mother leaving her only infant with a new babysitter for the very first time, Eddie laid out everything in great detail. How Secretariat hated the sound of motors and anyone fussing with his ears. How he loved his oats and cut-up carrots, even more than hay or sweets. How he loved to play with his halter, like a dog tugging on his own leash. How you could get him to lift a foot just by using your voice and asking nicely. How the sight of even one camera could get him posing and sticking out his chest, like a movie star.

"What will you miss about him?" someone asked Eddie.

"Early in the mornings," he replied. "Every morning at 5:30 Secretariat would be sitting there waiting for me. He and Riva Ridge would be waiting, looking down the shed row . . ."

Then the question came: "What will Secretariat miss most in his retirement?"

"He's going to miss running," Eddie said. "Every morning he would wait for someone to put the tack on so he could get out and run. He loved it."

During the week Eddie spent at Claiborne, the owner of that immense and legendary farm offered Eddie a job. The owner, of course, knew of Eddie's bond with the horse, and he must have thought that the best thing for Secretariat's health and well-being was to maintain the bond. For Eddie, the job would have meant staying in contact with his beloved Secretariat, work with regular hours, no more travel, and much more time with his family. But Eddie said no.

As much as he was devoted to Secretariat, he was also

Eddie sheds a tear on the day he says goodbye to Secretariat.

devoted to Lucien—who was like a second father to him. Lucien had employed him since he was fifteen years old, and Eddie could not leave him *or* the racetrack life. Nor did he want to uproot his family from New York. Eddie's wife and children had grown accustomed to his long absences from home as he drove horses from one racetrack to another. When it came down to choosing between a regular job and a racetrack job, Eddie went with the old and the familiar. Not even Secretariat could change his mind. So they went their separate ways, the muscled red horse and his muscled black groom.

On Eddie's last day at Claiborne Farm, Ray Woolfe took a shot that captured all the emotion and heartbreak of the day. Ray had taken thousands of photographs in both colour and black-and-white of Secretariat and the people on his team all through 1972 and 1973, but Ray told me that his two favourite shots are these: the black-and-white one taken on the plane showing horse and groom face to face, and the one of Eddie leaving Claiborne. That photo was taken from behind. He's standing by a low wall looking out to the fields, his overnight bag behind him. His left hand has come up to his face to wipe away a tear.

CHAPTER 12

LIFE AT CLAIBORNE FARM

Claiborne Farm is about as close to horse heaven as an earthly horse can get. The farm was started by Bull Hancock, a good friend to Christopher Chenery, Penny's father. Bold Ruler, Secretariat's sire, lived at Claiborne and is buried there. If you go to Claiborne today, you can see Secretariat's old stall. It's plenty big, with high ceilings. The black wood on the door is freshly painted and nicely sets off the plates screwed into it. In polished brass are the names of the great horses who once called this stall home: Unbridled, Easy Goer, Bold Ruler, Secretariat. That was a nice touch. Putting Big Red in his daddy's stall.

Nearby is Secretariat's old paddock, almost two acres in size. The fencing is black, the gate is yellow, and trees at the far end would have offered welcome shade in summer. Here the great Secretariat held court and posed for fans

Secretariat's new home at Claiborne Farm in Kentucky.

and their cameras. Ten thousand visitors came every year, with crowds especially heavy around the time of the Derby. One year, the farm closed its doors to the public because traffic made the normal running of the farm impossible. There were always champion horses here, but the visitors would almost always go straight for Secretariat.

About a year after Eddie surrendered Riva Ridge and Secretariat to Claiborne Farm, he went back to the farm to pick up a foal for Lucien Laurin. For Eddie, it was a chance to visit his old pals. He went to Secretariat's paddock, and the horse rushed to greet him and pulled on his shirt—"like he always did," Eddie later said. As for Riva

Ridge, Eddie offered an old greeting to the horse (it was a noise he used only with Riva), and Riva charged the fence so fast he almost slipped. Those horses didn't just remember Eddie. They ran to him like kids to a father who has been gone too long.

Eddie left secure in the knowledge that Secretariat was enjoying a pretty good life. Everything at Claiborne was, and is, first class. Consider these numbers. Size of the farm: 3,000 acres. Number of barns: 30. Number of stalls: 650. The farm has 90 miles of fencing and 27 miles of paved road. The entryway of cut stone and the gate of black iron say to all who enter that this is a grand place for grand horses. There are ponds, and swans in the ponds. You come, and you don't want to leave.

Every day Secretariat would be led out to his paddock. The grass was good, and he feasted on that until 2 p.m., when he was taken back to his stall. He would get two quarts of grain in the morning and twenty-five pounds of hay in his stall.

When he went to Claiborne, he was still just three years old, a very young horse. He may have missed his old job at the track, and some days he would race a fine horse called Round Table in the paddock next to his. They would sprint along the fence line that separated them, then break off. For two veterans of the track, it was as close as they could get to actual racing. Spring through fall, Secretariat would roll in the dust and the mud, and in winter he would lie on his back and kick at snowflakes as they fell. With visitors he would play stick like a dog.

His new job now, and he didn't mind it one bit, was in the breeding shed. Secretariat sired 663 foals in his fifteen years at Claiborne farm. He never did breed another Secretariat, and some people were surprised and disappointed by that. They shouldn't have been. A horse like Secretariat is like a comet in the sky. If you saw that comet streak, you were very, very lucky. Such a sight wouldn't be seen again for a long, long time, if ever.

Many of Secretariat's colts and fillies—especially his fillies—were outstanding horses. They won $29 million on tracks all over North America. Risen Star won the Preakness and the Belmont in 1988. Lady's Secret won more than $3 million. Charismatic, his grandson, won the Derby and the Preakness. Another grandson, Tobasco Cat, won the Preakness and the Belmont.

But there would be only one Secretariat.

He won a mittful of honours and trophies in his two years of racing. He was Horse of the Year in 1972 and again in 1973. He was Champion Two-Year-Old in 1972, and in 1973 *Sports Illustrated* magazine named him Athlete of the Year. He was Champion Grass Horse in 1973, the same year he won the Triple Crown—the Derby, the Preakness and the Belmont. He set world records in all three races, and those records still stand.

▼▼▼

All horses, all humans, must eventually take that final breath. Secretariat's time came at 11:45 a.m. on October 4, 1989. He was nineteen years old and still living the good life at Claiborne Farm. His many admirers, saddened by his death, wished that he could have died peacefully in his sleep, or suddenly—without a moment of pain or discomfort. Sadly, that was not the case. What took him is a horseman's nightmare: a painful disease of the hoof called laminitis, though "founder" is what most horsepeople call it. What causes the disease remains a mystery, but some veterinarians believe that too much grain or grass in the horse's diet might lead to it. Sometimes an infection can lead to blood poisoning, and that will bring on the disease.

Claiborne staff did everything they could to save him. For most of September, veterinarians treated Secretariat, and at one point they thought the disease was under control, but then he took a turn for the worse. He had the disease in all four feet, and there was nothing to be done. By this time, a groom named Bobby Anderson was looking after Secretariat. Just before noon on October 4, he led the horse into a van by his stall, and they gave him a needle to end his suffering. Bobby Anderson called it the saddest day of his life.

The news hit Eddie Sweat hard. He cried a long time and wouldn't eat. He told his closest friends that had he been there, he could have saved Secretariat. And maybe he could have. Eddie now regretted not taking that job at Claiborne, and he mourned the loss of his Secretariat for the rest of his life.

▼▼▼

Secretariat's body was placed in an oak coffin that measured six feet by seven feet and three feet high, and his body was wrapped in the yellow racing silks of Claiborne Farm, where he had spent the last sixteen years of his life. Secretariat's burial was private, with about twenty people present. One Claiborne worker who was there said that the burial felt "like a death in the family."

Gus Koch was then the stud manager at Claiborne and he stayed at the farm until eight o'clock that night handling interviews from radio stations all over the world. "By nightfall," he said, "the whole area around the grave was covered in flowers. It was an amazing sight."

When visitors pass through the proud gates at Claiborne Farm, they go down a road and pass a pond on their left. On the right, there's a little red-brick building with black shutters on the windows that serves as an office; Secretariat's stall and barn are just a little farther on. He's buried, along with many other worthy horses, in the grassy area behind the office. A tall and neatly trimmed hedge defines the place and offers the sort of quiet a cemetery requires.

Secretariat's grave and marker are the first, on the right. Like all the others, his is a low stone marker, the rough stone white and grey. But there's a part of the stone right in the middle that's been made smooth, and there, cut into the stone, are his name and dates. It looks like this.

Secretariat's gravestone at Claiborne Farm.

Nearby are the marker stones of other famous Claiborne horses, including two of the old champ's relations, Princequillo and Somethingroyal. It seemed fitting to place him close to his mother and grandfather. Princequillo's stone marker, covered in moss gone various shades of green and black over the decades, has aged beautifully. Bold Ruler, Secretariat's sire, is here too. He died in 1971, before his famous son had even run his first race.

▼▼▼

Eddie Sweat would die nine years after Secretariat did, in the spring of 1998, at the age of fifty-nine. But where the whole word mourned the horse, few seemed to notice the passing of his groom.

Eddie died poor, so poor that his sister, Geraldine—who had little money herself—had to pay for the funeral. Roger Laurin, Lucien's son, paid the airfare so Eddie's wife and children could fly from New York to the burial near Holly Hill, South Carolina. Eddie's house had been lost in a dispute with the government over taxes owed, and whatever money he had saved over the years mysteriously disappeared. Talk to Eddie's family and some will say that someone close to Eddie spent a large chunk of the money, while others say that Eddie was simply a wildly generous man—that he gave away money to racetrack friends and to family back in South Carolina. No one really knows what happened to Eddie's savings or why he died with nothing. Geraldine even had to buy her brother a blue suit so they could lay him out in his coffin with dignity.

This much is certain: the man who groomed a prince of a horse died a pauper. The only thing that Eddie had to pass on to his children was two acres of land in South Carolina.

Gone too were all the trophies and silver plates and all the things he had kept as a way of remembering his time with Secretariat. It's as if there had been a giant garage sale and every one of his possessions had been hauled away. How strange and sad that the man given the job of brushing the most valuable horse in the world died without a penny to his name.

Near the end of his days, Eddie almost surely had regrets. Had he taken the job that Claiborne Farm offered him in 1973, perhaps he could have saved Secretariat from the hoof disease that killed him. He must have had moments when he wondered why so little of the great wealth that Secretariat generated went the groom's way. On the other hand, Eddie took to his grave the knowledge that he was the only groom in history to have rubbed back-to-back Kentucky Derby winners, and that he had formed a remarkable bond with the greatest racehorse who ever lived. And you can't put a value on that.

When Eddie was a boy, people of his colour had to ride at the back of the bus and sit in the back of theatres. According to the rules of segregation then practised in the American South, people with black or brown skin weren't allowed in certain bars and restaurants. Black folk went to their own bars and restaurants; white folk had theirs. There were separate entrances for "Negroes" at baseball stadiums (there was even a Negro league, and black-skinned ball players weren't allowed to play alongside white-skinned ball players until Jackie Robinson broke the so-called colour barrier by playing with the all-white Brooklyn Dodgers in 1947). When Eddie Sweat was a boy, blacks and whites had separate schools, separate hotels, even separate drinking fountains. Slavery may have ended with the Civil War, but racism was alive and well. And so was poverty. The words *poor* and *black* seemed to go together, like peas and carrots.

Eddie was a black man from the old South, and whenever he was in the company of white people—and especially white people with money and power—he would listen politely, speak only when spoken to, put his hands in his back pockets and stare at the ground. Still, a little of Secretariat's shine had rubbed off on him. Eddie had earned enough money to buy a nice house in New York, and for a black man from South Carolina with little education that was a great accomplishment.

He had used his contacts to get his nephews jobs at the track, good jobs that paid far more than what they would get back home in South Carolina. Everywhere Eddie went, people stopped him and asked for his autograph. They had seen him on television, leading that magnificent horse. Eddie was on the cover of *Ebony* and *Jet*, magazines aimed at black readers.

Writers who had been around racetracks all their lives and who later wrote books on Secretariat praised Eddie to the heavens. Everybody loved Eddie and thought the world of him. One writer called him "the groom of grooms," and another described the bond between Eddie and Secretariat as the sweetest he had ever seen. Penny Chenery said that Eddie was "the finest man around a horse I ever saw." Eddie, she said, wasn't just part of the Secretariat team; he *was* the team.

Eddie had one dying wish: he wanted to have a place in the National Museum of Racing and Hall of Fame in Saratoga Springs, New York. The museum honours all the great horses, jockeys and trainers. Secretariat, of course, is there, and so are Ron Turcotte and Lucien Laurin. Penny Chenery is not there for the simple reason that owners play no active role in racing and therefore no owner has a place in the Hall. Eddie Sweat's name is not in racing's Hall of Fame either, because the work of grooms is not recognized.

Edward "Shorty" Sweat *should* be in racing's Hall of Fame. Maybe if enough of us write the museum, they'll reconsider. Grooms deserve to be recognized. And if Eddie belongs, so do a great many other grooms.

If you agree that Eddie does belong, write a letter to the Hall of Fame. Tell them why Eddie belongs inside, with his beloved Secretariat. Here's the address:

National Museum of Racing and Hall of Fame
191 Union Avenue
Saratoga Springs, New York
U.S.A. 12866–3566
e-mail: nmrmedia@racingmuseum.net

CHAPTER 13

THE MAIN CHARACTERS:
WHERE ARE THEY NOW?

▼▼

Although Secretariat is gone, he is clearly not forgotten. There are two life-sized bronzes of him in Lexington, at Kentucky Horse Park, and a third at Belmont Racetrack. In that one, he looks to be flying.

There is a website, Secretariat.com, where you can buy Secretariat hats and T-shirts and bobble-head dolls. There is a Secretariat chocolate bar; there is Big Red Gum. You can buy, if you like, a Secretariat Christmas tree ornament and a Secretariat fleece blanket. Posters and portraits of him still sell well. A postage stamp was created in his honour, and in Virginia there is talk of selling Secretariat licence plates to help raise money for a Secretariat museum. There is a big race named after him. There is even a farm for retired racehorses in his name.

But of all the things we have to remember Secretariat, two stand out. One is a big book, called *Secretariat,* by Raymond Woolfe that tells the life story of Secretariat in both words and photographs. Some of the most touching photos show Secretariat with Eddie Sweat. The other is the bronze at Lexington, by a Wisconsin sculptor named Ed Bogucki. He, too, understood what Eddie meant to Secretariat.

Ed Bogucki had originally imagined that his sculpture would show just the horse and his jockey. But when he saw the photographs of Eddie with Secretariat on the plane and of Eddie crying after delivering the horse at Claiborne, he changed his mind. The groom, the sculptor realized, deserved to be part of the bronze. Eddie had earned the right.

The sculptor had already met Secretariat. He had gone to Claiborne Farm in 1989, just months before the great horse died. Bogucki ran his hands over the stallion's body, and though the horse had aged and was carrying too much weight, he remained impressive. "He still had a lot of power," the sculptor said, "even though he was not running. You could feel the greatness. He oozed it." Bogucki took photographs and measurements.

Then the sculptor travelled to Saratoga Springs, where he met Ron Turcotte. More photos, more measurements. Eveything had to be just right.

Finally, Ed Bogucki got a message to Eddie Sweat. Would you please, he asked Eddie, come to Wisconsin and look over the clay model I've created? Of course, said Eddie, who

The bronze of Secretariat, Ron Turcotte, and Eddie Sweat is unveiled in Lexington, Kentucky in the summer of 2004.

rarely said no to anybody. The sculptor sent him plane tickets in the mail and later met him at the airport. At this point, Eddie had no idea that *he* was in the sculpture.

"You got my boots and my hat!" is what Eddie said as he approached the model. He was, of course, very surprised and very, very pleased. The bronze honoured a great horse, a fine rider and a devoted groom. Eddie saw the clay model but did not live to see the bronze unveiled in Lexington in the summer of 2004.

The statue captures the moment just after the running of the Kentucky Derby, when Secretariat was still hot and wired—"on the muscle," as horse people say. Ready to explode. Ron Turcotte is in the saddle, and he's watching to see what Secretariat might be up to. The horse's mouth is open, his neck is arched, and he looks like he could run another mile at the drop of a hat. And speaking of hats, Eddie, as always, is wearing his. He's got one hand on the reins at Secretariat's mouth, the other on the horse's body.

Ed Bogucki liked Eddie Sweat and admired him, and the two Eds even talked seriously about buying a horse together. At the unveiling, Bogucki told a story of working outside on the bronze when a gust of wind blew a heavy ladder towards the sculptor. The blow might have killed him. But the ladder, instead, struck Eddie. The bronze Eddie, that is. Eddie, in a way, had saved Bogucki's life.

▼▼▼

When the bronze was unveiled in Lexington, when the curtains were lifted and the trumpets blared, not everyone was there who should have been there. Some had died; some could not be found. But whether they were there to say a few words into the microphone or not, on one thing everyone in Secretariat's circle would agree: that horse had changed them all, marked them in some way.

Penny Chenery was at the unveiling. A tall, dignified woman in her early eighties, she looked healthy and bright. Before the speeches, scenes from Secretariat's life—including the Belmont—were shown on a big screen. Like many have done since, Penny tried to imagine what was going on in the mind of Secretariat as he ran that unforgettable race.

"I would love to know what he was thinking that day," Penny said. "Why did he keep on running when he'd passed everybody by almost an eighth of a mile? I just think he got out there and put away Sham early, and he said, 'Okay, I feel good, I'm just going to show them how I can run.'"

Penny thanked Secretariat's trainer, Lucien Laurin (Lucien had died in 2000, at the age of eighty-eight). To thank Lucien, Penny borrowed an expression from the horse world: a "made" horse is a fully trained horse. "Lucien made all of us," she said. "He made Ronnie; he made Jimmy; he made me." (She meant Ron Turcotte and Jimmy Gaffney.)

Finally, Penny thanked Eddie. "The other, really important part of Secretariat's life," she said, "was Eddie Sweat." She remembered how either Eddie or Charlie Davis, the exercise rider, would sleep outside Secretariat's stall at tracks all over North America. "I'm sure," she said, "they were a very important part of his sense of well-being."

▼▼▼

Eddie was there in Lexington, but only in bronze. Eddie had groomed horses almost to his last day on this earth. He had died of a failing heart, but those who knew him best talked of how that heart broke the day Secretariat died.

A friend of Eddie's, also a groom, put it well. He said that "a great horse had passed through him." Sometimes a groom who spends a long time with an extraordinary horse ends up putting that horse above everything—above himself, above family and friends. If Eddie were alive, he might say that falling for Secretariat was the best thing that ever happened to him, but he might also admit that he paid a price. Eddie connected at some deep level with the grandest horse in creation. And when that horse passed on, a part of his groom went with him.

▼▼▼

Jimmy Gaffney was at the bronze unveiling. He, too, had to fight tears as he said, "Secretariat changed my life forever. Every time I had the privilege to get on his back, I felt the incredible, awesome sense of power. It's a feeling I'll never forget."

Jimmy was among the first to ride Secretariat, and he knew right away the horse was special. He bragged about the horse to his wife and mother. His mother responded by sending him a white underpad (it goes beneath the saddle for extra comfort) with the word "Secretariat" knitted in blue letters. Jimmy then bought two blue saddle pads (a quilted cloth the saddle sits on) and stitched the horse's name on them as well. He even took home the saddle he normally put on Secretariat and used his leatherwork kit to carve out the name of the horse he was sure would make history. Jimmy did all this before the young horse ran his first race.

▼▼▼

Ron Turcotte was there to admire the bronze and to share some Secretariat stories. He made everyone laugh when he thanked Penny Chenery for holding the event on his thirty-first birthday. (He was, in fact, closing in on birthday number sixty-three.)

Horse racing is both thrilling and dangerous, and Ron Turcotte knows that better than anyone. Many jockeys and exercise riders have broken almost every bone in their bodies, but the injury they fear most is a broken neck or back that will put them in a wheelchair. On July 13, 1978, Ron Turcotte was riding a filly called Flag of Leyte Gulf when that horse's legs clipped the legs of a horse in front. The jockey—riding in what was for him race number 20,281— was hurled to the ground at forty miles an hour. Ever since then, he has used a wheelchair to get around.

No horse, Ron said that day in Lexington, could hold a candle to Secretariat. "He was a charming horse, a lovely horse, and we used to fight over who was going to get up on him. I could talk about him all day long."

People have told the jockey they had heard stories about Secretariat—about how mean he was, how spooky he was. "The truth is," said his old rider, "he never did a thing wrong. He was the kindest horse in the world."

CHAPTER 14

THE LEGEND LIVES ON

▼▼▼

The Secretariat story continues to endure long after his last race and long after his death. Remarkably, the horse is attracting a whole new generation of admirers, while those old enough to remember him find ways to keep their memories of him alive.

Jean DellaRocco is one admirer who will never forget Big Red. She was five years old when she first saw Secretariat. She doesn't need a bronze or a painting or a photograph to bring back his image. She has him in her head. It's like a piece of film or video, and she can run the tape whenever she wants.

Jean spent summers as a child at Saratoga Springs in upper New York State, and every weekend her sister, parents, aunt and grandparents went to the stakes races at the stately old Saratoga track. Secretariat was her childhood hero.

Secretariat checks out two shy young fans.

"He was so beautiful and strong," she says. "He was the real-life version of a storybook horse."

DellaRocco's memory, sad to say, is both bitter and sweet. She was there at Saratoga on August 4, 1973, when Onion won. A little girl had gone to see the horse of her dreams, and while she was thrilled to see him up close and in the flesh, her dream horse lost. Of course, she cried. What made it even more upsetting for her was that her grandfather—out of just plain mischief—had bet on Onion. The rest of the family had all bet on Secretariat. The story is still told in the DellaRocco family. They laugh about it now. They didn't then.

▼▼▼

Seeing a photograph of the great Secretariat helps bring him back, but anyone who actually took his photograph may feel an even deeper connection. In the offices at Kentucky Horse Park in Lexington, for example, is a series of photographs on one wall, all framed and in colour. They show Secretariat playing in his paddock at Claiborne Farm.

Photo #1. The young horse is upside down, all four feet in the air. He's kicking away, and tossing up a little dust. What a happy horse.

Photo #2. The middle image shows him starting to rise. He's up on his two front feet and any second now he will spring up. A show of power.

Photo #3. His front legs are apart and he's stretching out his head while shaking his entire body to shake off the dust. There's a lot of dust, to the right of him and behind him. A red horse dust storm.

The photographs were all taken by a resident of Saratoga Springs, a Dr. L. J. Hoge. He had seen Secretariat run in August of 1972 and become obsessed with him from that day forward. Every time that horse ran at Saratoga, Dr. Hoge was there with his camera. And he was there at Claiborne Farm in Kentucky to record the great horse enjoying a dust bath.

▼▼▼

Another way to keep alive the memory of a great horse like Secretariat is to ride a horse with Secretariat blood in his veins. Tobi Taylor was a typical horse-crazy eight-year-old girl in 1973 and the horse she adored was, no surprise, the gorgeous chestnut. She put Secretariat posters up on her bedroom wall; she bought magazines when he was on the cover. She also wrote a letter to the Breyer people urging them to start work on a Secretariat model. (Breyer is a company that makes six-inch-high plastic horses of certain breeds and individual horses. They're for kids and collectors. And maybe there were other letters like Tobi's, because Breyer did eventually make a Secretariat model.)

By 1997, Tobi Taylor was a young woman in her early thirties. She had by then owned several horses and was working for a horse trainer in Arizona who one day asked her to ride a chestnut horse called Twinkie. He was an older horse who had served as a breeding stallion, a showjumper and a polo pony. At that time, he was a trail horse, the kind of calm and wise older horse you want on group trail rides to help calm the more excitable younger horses.

Only later did Tobi realize that old Twinkie was actually a horse called Statesman—one of the first sons of Secretariat. Statesman's dam was a draft horse, so he would have been chunkier than Secretariat. Still, he was handsome. Young children would see the horses and riders heading out on the trail, and they would want the riders to stop so they could admire "the pretty red pony." The one with the famous father.

▼▼▼

Here is another girl, another devoted fan of a champion horse. Renee Attili would grow up to become an exercise rider at a Thoroughbred horse farm in Virginia. When she was a girl, she loved the ponies at the local fair and a nearby petting zoo. Then she saw Secretariat, and she fell for him.

"Secretariat," says Renee, "was the horse that made horses truly come alive to me when I was a young girl. He was the most majestic, noble, powerful horse that I had ever seen."

Later, as an exercise rider, she watched some video of one of Secretariat's workouts. Many horses, when they're galloping hard, make a distinctive sound as they take into their lungs huge amounts of air, part of the fuel for the gallop. The sound is not easy to describe, but BRRAAPP BRRAAPP BRRAAPP comes close. Secretariat was making that sound as he ran, and Attili thinks of him every time she hears that sound.

A good and skilled rider, as Renee is, would have observed Secretariat's gallop in the way that an artist views a painting. The artist can often spot things that others can't. And what Renee saw on that video was "truly something not of this world. The way he worked with such power, and at the same time easy, was simply awe inspiring."

One day she was asked to ride one of his daughters, a filly called Secretary's Story. "I felt like I was riding royalty," she said. "Riding her was truly an honour. She had a similar beauty and air about her. She actually had been born missing an eye, but, like her sire, she ran because she loved it."

▼▼▼

One of the best libraries on horse racing is in Lexington, at the Keeneland Racetrack. The Keeneland Library is a neat newer building of grey limestone, and its many tall wide windows gently curve at the top. Inside the library, the ceilings are high, the dark brown tables are long and polished, and the southern light comes pouring in. There are horse paintings on the wall, small horse bronzes everywhere, and just about every horse book, horse magazine and horse newspaper under the sun. If you ask the librarian to bring out all the files on Secretariat, the stack would be taller than you are.

Those files are full of stories. Everyone who ever got close to Secretariat never forgot the experience.

There was, for example, the woman who went to see him at Claiborne in 1985 and who was allowed to run her hands over his body, to be photographed beside him and to take away as a souvenir one of his horseshoes. She wrote about this experience in a magazine and described how one wall of her home is like a Secretariat wall of fame— with many photographs, and that horseshoe in a fancy box of polished wood and clear glass. "He lives on that wall," she says. "And in my heart."

There was the man who wrote a letter to a Kentucky newspaper describing the time he went to Claiborne and a foreman there let him walk Secretariat to his pasture. At the gate, the foreman turned the horse loose and both men watched as he "turned two laps at top speed around his playpen. What a spectacle!" the man wrote. "The world's greatest athlete 'doing his thing,' and I was there."

There is the story of a woman who had called in to a radio show when the subject was the most unforgettable moments on television. The woman said she had been walking to her seat in a restaurant when she saw Secretariat in full flight. That sight stopped her in her tracks. "I saw this animal run," she said, "and I realized I was seeing something I would probably never see again in my life, the way that animal moved and owned the racetrack."

▼▼▼

This is a Secretariat story not to be found in those fat files in the library at Keeneland Racetrack.

In July of 2004, the bronze statue of Secretariat, his jockey and groom was about to be unveiled inside a big white tent at Kentucky Horse Park. A kind of Secretariat fair had formed on the broad walkways outside the tent. People who were there to attend the unveiling could also buy Secretariat posters and paintings, Secretariat snow globes (those little plastic ornaments you shake to create a snow storm), Secretariat key chains and pencils and bobble-head dolls. Every kind of Secretariat souvenir was for sale. But the reason that hundreds of people had come from all over North America was to see the Secretariat bronze unveiled.

Under a hot Kentucky sun, people lined up outside the tent. Almost everyone in line had a story to tell—of watching Secretariat run, of seeing him at Claiborne, of chatting to Eddie or Ronnie. None had a story to match the one that Judy Jones could tell.

Judy lives on a horse farm in Michigan. She is an equine artist—one, that is, who makes a living drawing horses. And, of course, she has drawn Secretariat.

In 1973, Judy was only three years out of high school. She and all her horse-crazy friends (they all owned horses and competed in shows) went to the Arlington Park Racetrack on June 30 of that year to watch Secretariat run. Through friends of friends, they even got onto the backstretch and talked to Eddie Sweat. They asked him all kinds of questions, and the one thing Judy remembers from Eddie's answers is what Secretariat drank. Lucien Laurin didn't trust the water at these tracks all over the continent, so Secretariat drank only bottled water. They always took with them a supply of top-quality water. Only the best for the best horse.

The young women took many pictures that day of themselves with the famous horse. Unfortunately, the film in the camera failed to advance, so there is no photographic record of the meeting. Judy is still upset about that.

But there would be many other chances to be photographed with Secretariat. Judy and her friends would drive often from their homes in Chicago south to Claiborne to visit Big Red. There and back was eight hundred miles, so it was no small trip. At the farm, the artists would take pictures of Secretariat, record his measurements and, when that work was done, just hang out with a horse they treasured.

"We used to feed him peppermints," Judy said. "He loved peppermints." As a young horse, he had loved carrots. Now he had a sweet tooth.

One day, a groom at Claiborne asked Judy if she would take a photograph of him and the horse. In the paddock were Judy and her two fellow artists, the groom and Secretariat. Judy held the camera and prepared to take the shot. But in the meantime, Secretariat had spotted the mints in the hand of one of the women. The groom was standing near the horse, his face close to the horse's, posing for that shot—when the horse suddenly and forcefully lifted his head.

He was asking for (demanding, really) a peppermint. Imagine all the power in his demand. Unfortunately for the groom, Secretariat's head caught him right under the nose, like a blow from a boxer. The uppercut knocked the groom out, then down. His nose was broken and blood was everywhere.

One of the women grabbed Secretariat; the others ran for help. All was forgiven (though the poor groom later had to have surgery to repair his shattered nose).

Judy Jones remembers that moment clearly. But she also remembers feeling awe in Secretariat's presence. "I especially remember," she says, "how beautiful his head and neck and eye were. I'm sure he could have his moments, like any stallion, but he was a really sweet horse. He let us touch him and never, ever laid an ear back or lifted a foot."

A horse who pins his ear back or lifts a foot may be showing displeasure, but Secretariat was happy to be the centre of their attention. The ladies with the peppermints adored him. Many adored him then, and still do.

CHAPTER 15

DID YOU KNOW?

▼▼▼

The flip of a coin gave Penny Chenery the foal called Secretariat.

Penny owned Somethingroyal and another mare called Hasty Matelda. Ogden Phipps owned a stallion, Bold Ruler. The two owners agreed to share foals produced in breeding over a two-year period, but only three foals came, not four as expected. So they decided to toss a coin (this was in 1969). The winner would get the pick of the three foals. The loser would get the other two foals. Penny lost the toss but won Secretariat.

Some **Secretariat numbers**: Every registered Thoroughbred has a number tattooed inside the upper lip. Secretariat's was Z20660. At the Meadow in Virginia, where he was born, he stayed in a stall reserved for the colt or filly thought by farm staff most likely to succeed: stall 11. At Belmont (his "home" track in New York), he stayed in Barn 5, stall 7. Though he was heavier than most Thoroughbreds, his shoes were about average—size five. In a few of his races, Secretariat wore the number 1A, and artists who painted him racing liked to use that number. During the Kentucky Derby in 1973, Secretariat stayed at Barn 42, stall 21—the same one occupied by Riva Ridge, the winner in 1972.

Countless fans bet on Secretariat but never cashed in the ticket at the racetrack. They kept the Secretariat ticket as **a souvenir**. The value of those uncashed tickets? More than $100,000.

Eddie Sweat used to make a sound to Secretariat when he tacked him up before a race to let the horse know it was time to go to work. Sometimes the horse would nap before a race, so he needed **a wakeup call**. What was the groom's special sound? Eddie would say Qaaaack! Qaaaack! As if he were calling to a duck.

When Penny Chenery began to raise money for the Ed Bogucki bronze sculpture, she organized an online auction to sell items from her **Secretariat collection**. Here is what the highest bidders paid, in American dollars:

For a blanket Secretariat wore after his last race—$21,600.

For Secretariat's Belmont Stakes blanket—$43,000.
For Secretariat's Triple Crown bit and bridle—$28,000.
For Secretariat's tack box—$13,000.
Total raised—$336,675.

Jimmy Gaffney, one of Secretariat's exercise riders (Charlie Davis was the other), was among the first to realize that the big, gorgeous chestnut horse was going to make history. Jimmy would take care to be around whenever the horse had his shoes changed (every four to six weeks), and he would ask the farrier for the old ones. Jimmy figured that one day **Secretariat's horseshoe**s might be worth something, and he put away forty-nine of them. Not long ago, Jimmy sold one—for $40,000.
Weight of **Ed Bogucki's bronze** of Secretariat, Ron Turcotte and Eddie Sweat? 1,500 pounds.

Not all Secretariat foals were winners. Some were **spectacular failures**. A horse called Canadian Bound sold for $1.5 million. Another, called Grey Legion, sold for $550,000. Neither, as horsemen say, could run a lick.

A **Las Vegas nightclub** offered Penny Chenery a lot of money if Eddie Sweat would walk Secretariat on stage before an audience twice a day for fifteen minutes. How much money? $25,000.

Secretariat almost leaps as he makes his move in a race.

After Secretariat won the Triple Crown, the legendary Sands Hotel in Las Vegas built a special suite. It featured a luxurious 4,000-square-foot set of rooms with four bars, a game room, a pool, a sauna and four bedrooms. Its name? **The Secretariat Suite.** Both suite and hotel are gone now, demolished to make way for a new development.

Secretariat had **a great heart**. It wasn't just that he tried hard in every race and showed courage. His actual heart was magnificent. After Secretariat died, a veterinary surgeon examined his body in an attempt to understand what had caused the laminitis that killed him (it remains a mystery). When the surgeon looked at his heart, he was shocked. Secretariat's heart weighed about twenty-two pounds! It was twice normal size and a third larger than any horse heart the surgeon had ever seen.

Years later, after Sham died, the same surgeon examined his heart, too. Sham, remember, was the fine horse who was second to Secretariat in the Derby, was second to Secretariat in the Preakness and who sprinted with Secretariat for a mile in the Belmont before finally giving up. The surgeon noted that Sham's heart was almost the biggest he had ever seen, but Secretariat's was even bigger. Even in death, the surgeon observed almost sadly, Sham was second to Secretariat.

A Massachussetts professor named George Pratt once travelled to Claiborne Farm to look at Secretariat. An expert on how horses move, the professor filmed Secretariat running and then examined the film in slow motion. He concluded that **Secretariat had the most efficient stride ever measured**. Professor Pratt, like so many who saw the horse up close, was filled with awe at the sight of him. "He looked," said the professor, "like he would run through a stone wall. He is a mountain of muscle, a mountain of dignity, a mountain of aristocratic bearing—the most impressive live creature I have ever looked upon."

Although much has been written about Secretariat's kindness, he was also **full of mischief**. Secretariat once took a reporter's notebook right out of the journalist's hands and ducked back into his stall with his prize. Only when Eddie Sweat yelled at him, "Give the man his notebook back!" did the horse drop it in the straw. Another time he took

Eddie Sweat and exercise rider Charlie Davis look on as Lucien Laurin tightens Secretariat's girth.

Eddie Sweat's rake, grabbed the wooden handle with his teeth and started raking his own stall. In 1973, just before his last race in Toronto, Secretariat grabbed the hat of a fan who got too close and tossed it—with the fine aim of a basketball player—into a bucket of water. At Claiborne Farm in Kentucky, he would sometimes frighten visitors to his paddock by charging them at full speed and then, at the last second, turning away. Or he would approach visitors calmly, as if looking for a pat on the nose, and then shower them with a mouthful of grass.

The girth is the narrow leather piece that goes under the horse's belly and keeps the saddle in place. Secretariat was **so wide** that a custom-made girth had to be made for him. His girth as a three-year-old was 76 inches. His weight before the Triple Crown was a jaw-dropping 1,555 pounds. After those three races, he weighed 1,131 pounds—a loss of 424 pounds!

Horsemen are often superstitious, and there's an old poem that warns against buying horses with **too much white** at their feet. Various versions of the poem exist. There's this one:

One white sock buy a horse,
Two white socks try a horse,
Three white socks look well about him,
Four white socks do without him.

Or there's this one:

One white foot
Ride him for your life;
Two white feet
Give him to your wife;
Three white feet
Send him far away;
Four white feet
Keep him not a day.

Secretariat had three white stockings. So much for the "wisdom" in old poems.

Every year around the time of the Triple Crown races in May and June, on March 30 (the day he was born) and October 4 (the day he died), delivery vans pull up to Claiborne Farm with **bouquets for Secretariat's grave**. The flowers come from all around the world. The flowers are the same ones that are made into wreaths and put over the winning horse's shoulders. At Derby time, it's roses. For the Preakness, it's black-eyed Susans. For the Belmont, it's white carnations.

Some people believe in **the ghost of Secretariat**. In 2004, I was at the Meadow—the farm in Virginia where the famous horse was born—and I spoke with a mother and her teen-aged daughter who had kept foals at the farm in years past. Both women had spent many nights at the Meadow tending to newborn foals. The daughter, Whitney Jones, told me that she and many other people have heard late at night the sound of a horse galloping on the track at the farm. But there was never a loose horse or any way of explaining the sound of a lone horse galloping—and it was always heard at the same time, precisely 3 a.m.

I asked both Whitney and her mother, Sandra, about the story. Did it frighten them? Or was it a comfort to hear that sound?

"Well . . . it's kinda weird," Whitney said, and then she and her mother started laughing. Then Whitney offered this explanation for the sound of a single horse galloping in the dark. "It's the spirit of Secretariat," she said.

Eddie Sweat worked as a groom for some forty-four years, almost his entire life. And all that time he carried around from track to track **a tack box**—home to his brushes and hoof picks, his horse medicines and horse bandages. The box was like a big suitcase, and, after 1973, there was one more item inside. When you flipped open the tack box, you saw, taped to the lid, a colour photograph of the proud groom leading Secretariat back to his stall after the Kentucky Derby. Eddie has his left fist raised high in the sign of victory. That photo stayed in the tack box until 1998—the year Eddie died. For twenty-five years, he had carried it with him.

In another trunk at home, Eddie had neatly folded the clothes he had worn on Derby day: the checkerboard pants of white, black and red; the white jacket with the patches of blue at the shoulder; the cheery white hat. How many times did he touch those clothes and remember his beloved horse?

CHAPTER 16

THE OTHER "BIG RED"

▼▼▼

Everyone who was there that ninth day in June of 1973 for the 105th running of the Belmont, and anyone who has ever watched that race on television or on video, has the same reaction—a shiver of delight. You can watch the race over and over again—especially that last half mile when Secretariat pulls ahead as if he had wings—and the response is always the same. Your spine tingles, as if a small charge of electricity has passed through you.

Stories were told after the race about its impact. People had never seen anything like it, and they reacted in strange and wonderful ways.

A famous golfer of the time, Jack Nicklaus, was watching the race at home with friends, and he found himself on the rug pounding the floor and close to tears as Secretariat sprinted home. His friends thought Jack had lost a marble or two, for he hardly followed racing. Jack himself was bewildered by his own response to Secretariat's astonishing run, and he asked a friend of his—who did follow horse racing—to explain what had gotten into him. The friend told him, "Jack, all your life you've been aiming at perfection. And in that race, you saw perfection."

Pete Rozelle, head of the National Football League, was at the racetrack, up in the fancy section that features a bar and a restaurant. Everyone there was standing, cheering, and Rozelle—a very distinguished man, a proper gentleman—said that late in the race he felt someone's hands around his ankles. He thought maybe someone had fallen. Then he looked down and he realized he was standing on a table! And he had no idea how he got up there.

That day Secretariat was not running *into* the wind. Secretariat *was* the wind.

Penny Chenery later said that if there was one moment she would want Big Red remembered for, it was the Belmont Stakes. "Really," she said, "he was running that fast just out of the joy of running. Not from the whip, not from competition. He was running because he loved it."

Penny had noticed how playful Secretariat was after workouts and how running made him happy. "It is as if he thinks," she said, "racing is a game we thought up for his amusement."

His winning a race by thirty-one lengths got some racetrack writers thinking of another horse, a legendary horse who also bore the nickname Big Red. That horse, Man o'War, once won a race by a hundred lengths. And so began the debate that continues to this day. Who is the greatest racehorse of all time? Is it Secretariat, or Man o'War? If you could, by some wizardry, put the two horses in a race, who would win? Secretariat? Or Man o'War?

▼▼▼

Two horses, decades apart and, in some ways, very different. And yet, in many other ways, they were very much alike.

First, the differences. Man o'War raced in another time, just after the First World War. He wore heavy steel shoes during races, while Secretariat wore the light aluminum shoes that came later. There was no starting gate in Man o'War's days, for it had yet to be invented. Instead, horses simply lined up behind a long rope or webbing (a little like a volleyball net) and when the barrier was pulled up and away, the race was on. Man o'War was quite fiery before races, unlike Secretariat, who was usually calm.

But look at how similar they were. Man o'War was a muscled chestnut, like Secretariat, with markings much like Secretariat's. Both horses caught the attention of the world and gave Americans, especially, cause to smile. In Man o'War's time, a majestic horse offered relief to a people made sad and anxious by the horrors of the First World War. Secretariat did the same when war and scandal troubled all Americans. Both Man o'War and Secretariat were called

Top: Man o'War and jockey.
Bottom: Secretariat and exercise rider Charlie Davis.

"the horse of the century." Both had big strides and even bigger appetites. Both horses were groomed by black men from the American South. Man o'War's groom for fifteen years was Will Harbut, who would entertain the fifty thousand visitors who came every year to Faraway Farm outside Lexington to see the horse and hear Harbut's stories. Man o'War adored Will Harbut, as Secretariat loved Eddie. Both horses won races by fantastic margins: Man o'War's margin of victory in one race was a hundred lengths (there was just one other horse in that race, a rather ordinary horse who was likely still tired from racing the day before). Both Man o'War and Secretariat ran twenty-one races, and each ran his last race in Canada.

When Man o'War died at the age of thirty—a ripe old age for any horse, let alone a racehorse—his funeral was broadcast live on national radio. Some two thousand people came to his burial, most of them in tears. They filed past his open coffin—a six-foot by ten-foot oak casket lined in Faraway Farm's black-and-yellow racing colours—and many reached down to touch him.

The death of Man o'War was front-page news around the world, just as Secretariat's death was. When Secretariat died, flags in Lexington flew at half-mast, and when Man o'War died, the windows of storefronts all over Kentucky were edged with black wreaths.

A much-admired track writer in the time of Man o'War said of the horse, "He was as near to a living flame as horses ever get, and horses get closer to this than anything else." One racetrack official who helped start many of Man o'War's races said the horse was "so beautiful it almost made you cry, and so full of fire that you thanked your God you could come close to him." Many said much the same thing of Secretariat, and those ten thousand fans who trooped every year to Claiborne all had the same questions: Can I see him? Can I take his photograph? Can I touch him?

Every few years, some of racing's newspapers, magazines or broadcasters like to stir up the old debate, Man o'War versus Secretariat. Who would win that race? Impossible to say for sure, since tracks were slower then, horses carried different weights and wore different shoes, so you can't simply compare race times. You're comparing apples and oranges. In the Man o'War versus Secretariat debate, it's a matter of opinion.

After Secretariat's win in the Belmont, a trainer named Holly Hughes—so good he made Thoroughbred racing's Hall of Fame—said he had seen all the great horses, including Man o'War, and none could compare with Secretariat. "You have," he told Lucien Laurin, "the greatest horse in the history of racing."

Charles Hatton, the great racetrack writer (it was he who invented the term "Triple Crown" to describe the Derby, the Preakness and the Belmont), had also seen both Man o'War and Secretariat race. One time he went back to Secretariat's barn at Belmont Racetrack and he asked Eddie to bring the horse out so he could look at him. Charles Hatton just stared at the horse for a full five minutes, saying nothing all that time. He was stunned into silence. An old black trainer, a former slave, had taught Hatton all about horse conformation—how the lines should go at the neck and the shoulder and the knee—so he knew what the perfect horse should look like. But no horse was perfect. Every horse had a flaw, most had several, and some had many. Not this one. Charles Hatton the writer, like Jack Nicklaus the golfer, was looking at perfection.

Some surveys in racing magazines have ranked the best racehorses of all time, putting Man o'War first and Secretariat second. Were he still alive, Charles Hatton would have rejected the thought. Secretariat, he once said, is "the greatest I have seen and the greatest anyone has ever seen." And a lot of people agree with him.

In 1999, the television network ESPN put together a list of the top fifty athletes of the twentieth century, and only one animal made that list: Secretariat. That same year, *Time* magazine ranked the ten most influential athletes of the twentieth century. The baseball player Babe Ruth was on that list, and so was the basketball player Michael Jordan. As was the racehorse Secretariat.

When Secretariat raced in the Derby, the Preakness and the Belmont, he set a world record in each race. Those records stand more than thirty years later. Some experts are convinced that no horse will *ever* break his times. And so to call Big Red "the horse of the century," you have to wonder if that name will still apply next century, the one after that, and in the ones to follow.

Those who know the sport of racing can look at a certain race's distance, note the time of the winning horse and understand in a heartbeat just how good that horse was. Secretariat's numbers are off the scale. But the stopwatch alone fails to capture his greatness. He touched a lot of people (Eddie Sweat not least among them), and no horse has come along to take his place. The way he won races, the pure joy he seemed to take from running, his stunning good looks, all earned the big red horse a place in the human heart and in racing history.

BIOGRAPHY OF PHOTOGRAPHER
RAYMOND WOOLFE

▼▼

Born in New York City in 1935, Raymond Woolfe became a professional steeplechase rider at the age of sixteen and still holds the record as the youngest rider ever to earn victory at a major American race track—Saratoga. In 1970, Raymond Woolfe became head photographer for the *Daily Racing Form* (DRF), a newspaper that covers Thoroughbred racing in North America. It was during this time that he recorded—in words and photographs—Secretariat's life and career. He went on to write a book called *Secretariat*, which became a best-seller, one that continues to sell to this day. Raymond Woolfe lives at Hawk's Nest Farm, near Charlottesville, Virginia.

ACKNOWLEDGMENTS

▼▼

The Big Red Horse owes a great debt to several people at HarperCollins: editorial assistant Patricia Ocampo, designer Sharon Kish, and managing editor Noelle Zitzer.

I am grateful, as well, to two freelancers: copy editor Shaun Oakey and proofreader Cathy Witlox.

My deepest thanks go to Lynne Missen, executive editor of children's books at HarperCollins, who guided this manuscript home. Edward "Shorty" Sweat had a touch with horses; Lynne Missen has a touch with writers.

Several readers saw this book in an early form, and offered timely suggestions and much valued encouragement: Ulrike Bender, the best in-house editor a man could hope for, and Bryn Davis, a young reader who was also kind enough to invite me into her classroom—my riding gear in tow. I thank my son, Kurt Scanlan, too, though he had nothing to do with this book. I just like to see his name in print.

Raymond Woolfe eloquently chronicled the life of Secretariat in both words and photographs, and I am grateful for his permission to reproduce some of those gorgeous pictures here.

My agent, Jackie Kaiser, belongs on this page for all that she does for me. I like to see her name in print too.

Finally, I am grateful to the man and the horse who inspired this book: Eddie Sweat and his beloved Secretariat. Each brought joy to the other, and it was a joy to write a book that strives to honour them both.

—Lawrence Scanlan